Dedicated to readers everywhere.

Also by Maureen Turner

First Breath: Hardback/Paperback and eBook

Do Androids Dream?: e book

Purgatory: e Book

Kindlebooksbymaureen.co.uk

MAUREEN TURNER

FANTASY ROMANCE NOVELIST

WINGS UNFURLED

Books One and Two

Malchediel-Warrior Angel

And

Amy-Nephilim Freedom Fighter

MALCHEDIEL – WARRIOR ANGEL

BOOK ONE

"I'm an Angel. I can do things that mortals can only dream of."

Contents

Prologue

Malchediel was the first to land, his right foot making contact with the ground fractionally before his left. He grinned as he steadied himself determined not to take any ungainly steps forward as he balanced himself. Like an athlete dismounting from the high bars or the horse during an exercise he always schooled himself to make a perfect landing. His wings which had been beating at their full extent slowing him as he touched down, now beat once, twice, and stilled, folding neatly against his back. He leaned forwards, hands on hips attempting to control his rapid breathing whilst looking over his right shoulder waiting for his friend Nemamiah to land. His grin broadened as the second angel tumbled from the sky to land heavily a few feet from him. His wings too were beating rapidly attempting to put the brake on his much faster descent. He staggered three or four strides before planting both feet firmly beneath him. He looked over to Malchediel sheepishly who was now sniggering at his companion's ungainly landing. Nemamiah sheathed his sword still wet with demon blood before smiling at his own less than perfect return home.

"Okay, okay, we can't all be perfect...besides the sword was heavy; I notice you weren't encumbered with any weapons." At this Malchediel laughed out loud as he reached out pulling his friend towards him just in time to avoid a collision with the third and fourth angels who were plunging from the skies. Qaphsiel and Paschar made contact simultaneously still arguing about which of them had cast the fatal blow sending the last of the demons back to hell. Straightening, Malchediel looked Nemamiah up and down taking in his bloodied cropped trousers which were completely torn down his left thigh and only held together by the waistband. All four angels were breathing rapidly, their hair plastered to their heads. It had been a hard battle. They had

"Wow! That had to have hurt," said the stunningly attractive individual. The comment could have been taken as compassionate and heartfelt had it not been accompanied by a grin. Her embarrassment was acute as was her irritation that he found it funny.

"I'll survive." she said shortly glaring at him. His smile widened. He was clearly finding the situation very amusing. He surveyed her making her feel even more uncomfortable. "I didn't hear you come in." she uttered, instantly regretting having to account for being caught under the table. "Is there something I can help you with?" she added taking in his tousled sun-bleached hair. *Clearly another of those over-confident surfers...Bet he doesn't spend anything.* He casually looked around him taking in the entire contents of the shop. Without looking at her he asked, "Is it okay to browse around?" Unhurriedly he turned back to her and she was aware of how startlingly blue were his eyes. The grin had subsided but there was still a definite upward lift to the corners of his mouth.

"Of course." she answered acutely aware that perhaps she was staring. She had never seen him before so he was certainly not a local. She would have remembered those eyes. She turned away attempting to convince him that she regularly had stunners like him wandering around the shop. After a few minutes she surreptitiously glanced across at him. He had his back to her examining one of her Gunwalloe Cove seascapes. He was broad-shouldered; indeed he had the build of an athlete. His hair was the colour of sun warmed sand, an enviable golden blonde that curled softly against his face, hanging well past his collar. Almost as if he knew he was being observed, he turned and met her eyes. She hastily looked away then realised that by doing so made it all the more obvious that she had clearly been watching him. She expected him to grin at her again; he without a doubt enjoyed her discomfiture, but this time there was no lordly smirk, "How much is this one?" he asked indicating the Gunwalloe. She would have been happy with fifty pounds for it. "One hundred and twenty five pounds."

she answered.

"Fine, would you put it to one side for me. I'll call back this afternoon for it." He said without hesitation.

Yeah…right. She thought. *That's the last I'll see of you,* but she answered pleasantly enough, "Certainly, I'll hold it until tomorrow for you."

He held her gaze for a moment before turning for the door. "By the way," she called after him. "I didn't catch your name."

"That's because I didn't give it to you." Again that amused grin. "But it's Divine." He walked back towards her holding out his hand which after a moment's hesitation she took. His handshake was firm and she quickly took in his long fingers and incredibly clean, manicured nails. "But you can call me Mal."

For some unaccountable reason she felt momentarily flustered. He released her hand and turned back towards the door commenting over his shoulder, "And I **will** be back later." At the door he turned and looked back and smiled at her but this time without the underlying smirk, then opening the door he went out. She stared at the closed door and the swinging little bell above it. She was now more convinced than ever that she had not heard it ring when he had entered the shop. In spite of herself she hoped that he would keep his promise and return later and that hope wasn't just to clinch the sale of the painting.

Once outside the shop Malchediel paused looking down at his right hand…the hand that had shaken hers. His fingers were tingling and that had never happened during previous odd encounters with mortals. This girl was definitely different from normal human beings. Raguel had said that she knew nothing about her supernatural powers…how on earth was he going to help her come to terms with being different from everyone that she knew, and how was he going to teach her to protect herself in the future?

After he left the shop Amy carried on with securing

hanging twine to the back of her new canvases and then proceeded to re-arrange the display leaving the Gunwalloe Cove picture on the bench even though she wasn't altogether sure that she would ever see the stranger again. He had stressed the word 'will' when he had said that he would be back almost as though he had detected her negative thoughts.

During the morning her thoughts kept returning to the stranger. Her first impression of him wasn't favourable. He had annoyed her by finding it funny that she had bumped her head. What made it worse was that it had been his fault. How the hell had he entered the shop so quietly. To make matters worse it had been embarrassing to be found crawling about under the table on hands and knees especially by a 'looker like him. His smirk as their eyes had met – he standing looking down at her and she still kneeling on the floor-had put her at a disadvantage. At that point she really hadn't like him. He had a superior air about him. Then again he had agreed to buy one of her paintings at a greatly inflated price, and he had stressed that he would be back to pick it up later. At this point she felt her animosity towards him waning a little. Finally the smile he had bestowed on her at the doorway had dispelled her first impression of him as an overconfident insensitive bore. She was willing to re-assess her opinion of him but that could only be achieved if and when he returned.

At mid-day Stephen from the Butcher's shop on the corner called in to see if she wanted him to pick up a sandwich from the Bakery for her lunch. He often called in during his lunch break offering to fetch her something to eat. She knew that he had a hidden agenda for these regular acts of kindness. A girl knew when a guy fancied her. Unfortunately for Stephen the feeling wasn't reciprocated. She liked him but that's as far as her feelings for him went. It was difficult to dissuade him from his obvious infatuation without hurting his feelings or worse still, alienating him to the point of turning his friendship into hostility. "Do you know Stephen, I have an awful headache.

I think I'll shut up shop for an hour and get some fresh air." She said, her fingers going to the bump under her fringe which was feeling quite tender and was clearly the cause of the throbbing ache. His face instantly took on a look of concern. "Do you want me to get some paracetamol from the Chemist for you?" He asked.

She smiled at him, "No thanks. I've already taken a couple of pain-killers. I just need a walk in the fresh air. Hopefully that will clear it." She didn't go into details of the bump on the head; he would probably have insisted that she lie down while he gently massaged her temples. "Okay." He said brightly, "I'll walk with you as far as the Bakers. Joe wants a pasty anyway." He leaned against the counter whilst Amy reached for her handbag. After locking up the shop they both strolled together along Falmouth High Street heading for the Bakery. "Are you going to get a sandwich or don't you feel like eating at the moment?" Stephen asked, but before she had chance to answer he carried on, "when I have a bad headache I don't feel like eating." She smiled at him and said that she would probably get a sandwich and after a walk along the harbour hopefully the headache would have gone and she would make a cup of tea back at the shop and eat it later. She was glad that Joe, Stephens' employer had ordered a pasty, that meant that Stephen would have to go straight back to the butchers where he worked before it got cold. She wasn't in the mood for small talk at the moment. The headache was beginning to subside and a solitary walk back to sit quietly at the harbour should make her feel better. Stephen let her choose her sandwich before he ordered two pasty's to be warmed in the micro-wave oven. She paid for her order and after saying goodbye to Stephen she left the shop alone and walked back the way they had come turning left down to the harbour. She found an empty bench and sat 'people-watching' in the warm September sunshine. It was something she had enjoyed doing with her late father and thinking about her dad bought a momentary feeling of sadness to her. He had died a little under two years ago after falling from a ladder whilst re-aligning the rooftop television aerial. Such a pointless accident, he was always so careful with his and Amy's safety. To die in such banal circumstances didn't make any sense. His death had left Amy a seventeen year old orphan. Her mother had been killed in a road traffic accident when Amy was only three years old and her memories of her Mum therefore had been very hazy. Sitting here on the harbour-side bench Amy let her thoughts roam back to the days before her fathers' accident. He had often spoken to her of her mother and he had confided in her that there were things that he had kept from her as she grew up, things that involved her mother that perhaps she ought to know about but not until she was 'grown -up'. The last time he had spoken thus was when she had been sixteen and she had insisted that at such a great age she surely must be old enough to hear what he had to tell her. He had stroked her face tenderly and said that she was still too young to see what he had to show her which made her think that perhaps he had mementoes that he wanted to pass on to her. "When you are eighteen, sweetheart, I will tell you all." When she was about to protest, he had silenced her with a finger on her lips, a loving smile and the words, "Don't try to grow up too quickly Amy. Enjoy your childhood." She had pouted claiming that she was no longer a child and he had laughed at her indulgently. They had never spoken of the 'secret' again and of course with his death it had all become irrelevant anyway. Once she had recovered from the shock of losing her father she had tried to discover what it was that he had kept secret for so long. She reached her eighteenth birthday six months after his death and this momentous occasion prompted the decision to rummage through the loft above their small cottage for any clues as to what the mystery was. She had found a large wicker trunk full of what must have been her mother's clothes. She sat for some time with the lid open just looking at the neatly folded garments marvelling at the reasons why her father had never disposed of them after so many years. Eventually she steeled herself to start going through the assortment of dresses, jumpers and trousers that her mother had once worn. Because she barely remembered the woman who had given birth to her it wasn't as traumatic as when she had packed away her father's things after his death. All his things had gone to the local charity shop. She wasn't sure what to do about the contents of the trunk. She sat on the bare boards of the loft and lifted each article out one by one, shaking them gently and trying to make a picture in her mind of the mother she couldn't remember. She even held some items close to her nose to see if there was a scent of her that may trigger long buried memories but all she detected was a musty fragrance of fabric long left un-aired. After half an hour there was a mound of clothes beside the trunk and she now came to a small wooden box, the lid inlaid with tiny sea shells. She smiled to herself, this box had lain inside the trunk for fifteen years but these little trinket boxes were still being sold in Cornish gift shops by the hundreds each summer. As she carefully lifted it out, two of the little shells dislodged and fell back into the trunk. Opening the lid of the box she peered at its contents closely. There was an assortment of earrings, a couple of bracelets, a wedding ring and a strange looking little charm. She held it in her hand and almost dropped it back into the box. Shockingly the charm started to warm up in the palm of her hand. It was so unexpected that she felt the hairs on the back of her neck stand up, then just as suddenly the charm cooled down and lay totally inert in her hand. Had she imagined it? She wasn't sure. She turned it over trying to make out what it was. It looked like a figure but it was too dim up in the loft to be sure. She placed it carefully in the back pocket of her jeans to examine later downstairs. All that was left in the trunk now were three pairs of shoes, all flat heeled. It got her to wondering if her mother had been tall. She herself was five foot seven and she found that if she wore heels she occasionally towered over some of the boys that she had dated .This little insight made her smile because she too often wore flat heeled shoes. She felt a sudden affinity to the woman whose clothes now lay in a heap besides her. She sighed and began to carefully put the folded clothes back into the trunk. Her father had kept them for so long that she thought it would be disloyal to his memory to dispose of them now. Once they were all back inside the trunk she lowered the lid, stood up, flexing her muscles which had stiffened up from sitting so long on the hard boards before making her way to the loft opening. She descended the steps after switching off the loft light and lowered the trap door back in place.

She was suddenly bought back to the present by the church clock chiming one. She looked quickly at her watch to check. It was indeed One o'clock. She had been sitting on the harbour bench for over half an hour lost in thought. She felt for the small silver charm that now hung around her neck. As she stood up to make her way back to the shop with her purchased sandwich her mind wandered back again to the day when she had found the charm. It had been later that same evening when she remembered that it was still in her back pocket. Taking it out she had held it under the desk lamp to examine it closely. It turned out to be a small angel about four and a half centimetres in length. It was exquisitely fashioned; the wings so delicate that using a magnifying glass she could make out the feathers etched on the surface. The face was incredibly sad. The eyes looked as though they may have been tiny diamonds but could just as easily have been glass. She had no idea if there was any value to it but she liked it so she had bought a silver chain from the local jewellers and threading it through the ring on the head of the angel she decided to wear it. Her father had never shown any inclination towards religion and she herself had never attended church so the attraction of the little charm held no ecclesiastical relevance. She just liked it and so had worn it ever since.

She made her way back up the slight incline onto the High Street and turned right heading back to the shop. Her headache had gone and she was now feeling hungry. As the shop came into view she was surprised to see the stranger standing waiting outside. He was casually leaning with his back against the wall to the right of the doorway, his right leg bent, with the sole of his shoe against the wall. He hadn't seen her yet and she quickly moved into the doorway of the bookshop and then peered around the edge of the window frame so that she could see him without being seen in return. He was eating an apple, clearly waiting for her return. He was casually watching the passers-by as they walked past him. As she stood surveying him an elderly man approached him with a small terrier type dog on a lead. As they were about to pass him the dog stopped and began to jump up against the strangers legs, clearly excited and wagging its tail. The owner appeared to be apologising as he pulled on the lead but the stranger was smiling and saying something to him which Amy couldn't hear from her vantage point but it was clear from the owner's answering smile that the stranger wasn't annoyed by the dog's enthusiastic prancing. He bent forwards and fondled the dog's ears then straightening up spoke again to the elderly man who appeared to laugh in return before moving off. So he had a fondness for dogs...she appreciated that. Left alone the stranger carried on eating his apple. She didn't delay any longer but stepped out from the bookshop doorway and walked the few yards towards her own shop. At her approach he looked up and seeing her smiled.

"I'm sorry," she said "have you been waiting long?"

"Oh about a couple of hours. That's all."

She glanced up at him detecting a slight uplift of his lips. "Funny," she answered, "you don't strike me as being the patient type."

"Do I not? What type do I strike you as being?" he asked taking another bite of the apple. This was getting into uncomfortable territory. She changed the subject. "I haven't had time to wrap up your purchase yet." she said inserting the key into the door. He turned the apple around taking one last bite before answering. "No matter." He said following her into the shop, "Another few minutes is neither here nor there."

She dropped her bag and sandwich on the workbench and then pulled a sheet of brown wrapping paper from the roll tearing it along the serrated blade. Lifting the canvas she placed it on-top of the paper but before she had time to wrap it, he bent over the bench to look at it. "Where is this Gunwalloe Cove?" he asked. "It looks very beautiful."

She paused holding the paper away from the painting as they both looked at it together. "It is. It's a bit off the beaten track so I often paint around that area. Off season it's very quiet so it's ideal from an artist's perspective."

"Is it far from here? I wouldn't mind seeing it for myself."

"Not at all. Take the Helston Road, the A394, and then turn right onto the A3083 as though heading for the Lizard. After about a mile you'll see a sign on the right for Gunwalloe."

"Helston, Lizard, Gunwalloe. I think I can remember that." He said straightening. "Do you mind if I throw this in your bin?" he asked holding up the apple core.

"No...the bin is over there." She answered nodding towards the counter as she commenced wrapping the canvas. He wandered over to the counter and dropped the core into the bin. "By the way how is the sore head?"

She glanced up at him wondering if she would see that sardonic grin again but this time he returned a completely neutral look. She turned her attention back to what she was doing. "Its fine...thanks." She said quietly. She finished wrapping the canvas in silence and held it out to him. "That's one hundred and twenty five pounds please."

He reached into his back pocket and counted out the correct number of notes handing them to her.

"Thank you Mr..."

"Just Mal." He said tucking the painting under his arm. He was about to leave the shop and it occurred to her that she would probably never see him again and for an instant she panicked at the thought. She knew she would regret it if she let him leave like this

"Mal?" she said in a rush, "Is that short for Malcolm?" Instantly she regretted such a stupid question because there was that sardonic grin again.

"Do I look like a Malcolm?" he asked teasingly. He really did have the knack of turning the tables on her.

"To be honest, no you don't."

He nodded thoughtfully, "Good, because my name is Malchediel."

"Mal-key-dee-ell." She repeated slowly, "I've never heard that name before. It's clearly not English."

His smile broadened, "No it's an ancient biblical name. Aramaic I believe."

"Oh." She said simply. There wasn't much else she could say to such a statement. He turned back to leave and as his hand went to the door handle she said in a rush, "You don't live around here...are you just in Cornwall for the surfing?"
He didn't turn back to her immediately and she had the embarrassing notion that he was grinning at her obvious attempt to keep him talking. What the hell was the matter with her? Just let him go. If he had any inclination to make small talk he would have done so. She was making herself look ridiculous. As he turned back to her she mumbled, "Sorry...silly question...any idiot knows that the best surfing is on the north coast." She was acutely aware that he could probably see her face colouring in embarrassment. She made herself look at him expecting to see him smirk at her clumsy attempt to keep him there but was surprised to see that his face showed no hint of amusement, indeed he appeared to be looking not at her face but at the angel charm hanging around her neck. Her hand instinctively went to it. The movement caused him to look at her face. "Erm...No, I don't surf. I'm just travelling around." There was no grin, no smirk, no sign of his being amused by her endeavour to delay his leaving. "That effigy," he said, indicating

the angel with a slight nod of his head, "is... unusual. Is it very old?"

She was surprised that he had noticed it but at least she had got him talking. "It was my mothers."

He said nothing but continued to look at her with what she felt was a renewed interest. "She died when I was quite young." She added to break the lengthening silence.

"And she left it to you?" he asked after a moment.

"In a way, I suppose." She answered. "I found it among some of her things about a year ago and decided to wear it as a necklace. I thought it was a pretty little charm."

His eyes dropped back to the angel. He frowned as he momentarily chewed the inside corner of his lip in thought. Lifting his eyes to her face he said, "Amy that's not a charm. It's a talisman, a juju, a thing of bad, not good luck." He could see that his words had startled her. Her face hardened.

"And you would know about these things would you? And how do you know my name anyway?"

"What? Oh...I was talking to someone outside while I was waiting for you and he asked if I was waiting for Amy...and yes I do know about religious artefacts as it happens." He added. "I studied theology."

"Oh." She said lamely. "Well..." she added, "It's a good job I'm not superstitious then isn't it?"

He decided to change the subject. He had been sent to protect her and he was confident that his powers were superior to those of an amulet so he let the matter drop...for now. He smiled at her. "Do you know I've already forgotten your directions to Gunwalloe? I don't suppose you would like to take me there sometime would you?"

When he dropped the cynical grin, his normal smile was very attractive and she felt herself warming to him again but he was still a stranger to her and she wasn't likely to offer lifts in her car to anyone she didn't know. "Helston, Lizard, Gunwalloe. Not too difficult even for a theology graduate." Now it was her turn to smirk.

beneath his feet. After a few seconds he re-appeared looking down at her from above and she caught her breath as he deftly jumped back down onto the beach a few feet away from her. It had to be twenty feet at least but he tackled the leap as though it were no more than two or three. "Your mouth is open again Amy." He said with a grin.

"Will you stop saying that?" She retorted. "What were you doing up there anyway?"

"Checking out a theory." He answered. He reached for her hand and led her away from the rubble. "Come and sit down and I'll explain all of this to you." He lowered himself to the sand and still holding her hand indicated that she sit with him. She paused momentarily then knelt down in front of him. Withdrawing her hand from his she looked at him expectantly.

"I didn't come into your shop earlier this week by chance." He began. "I was sent to protect you because it was felt you may be in danger."

"So you're like a guardian angel then?"

A wry look crossed his face. "Not exactly Amy, You have been under the scrutiny of a couple of guardian angels for some time…"

"I don't think so." She said, "I would have noticed. You're not exactly inconspicuous you know."

He smiled. "I'm not a guardian. I was sent because they have not been heard from since they started their mission. Guardians are very rarely seen so you wouldn't have known anything about their being here."

"So you are saying that they are invisible but you're not…So what sort of angel are you then?" Before he had chance to answer she rushed on, "Are you one of those Archangels?"

He laughed and she thought she had never heard such a melodious sound. "Heavens no! There are only seven Archangels and they rarely appear on Earth. The last time that happened was two thousand years ago. I'm a Warrior…I fight evil. With two Guardians down, Raguel thought it prudent to send someone more skilled to deal with this situation."

"Raguel?" she repeated, "who's Raguel?"

"He's a sort of Overseer."

"So why am I attracting the attention of Heavenly beings anyway?"

He hesitated before answering. "It seems that for the past year or so your aura has been smouldering with unhallowed shadows."

"You're beginning to lose me now. I'm still trying to get my head around Guardian, Warrior and Archangels and then you hit me with auras and unhallowed shadows."

He gave an exasperated "Hmmph." He took a breath and tried again. "Remember when I asked you about that Angel talisman around your neck earlier this week?"

She nodded.

"You said that you had found it amongst some of your mother's things."

She nodded again.

"How long did you say you had been wearing it?"

"I'm not sure...about a year I think."

He regarded her solemnly allowing what she had said to sink in. After a few seconds her hand flew to her mouth. "The same time as my wonky aura thingy!" she exclaimed through her fingers.

"Exactly."

They sat looking at one another and then she said, "It has to be a coincidence. The angel was my mothers. Why would she have passed on something harmful to me...it doesn't make sense."

"But she didn't pass it onto you Amy. Did she? You found it. Perhaps it had been hidden from you because your parents realised that it was evil."

"But then why wasn't it just destroyed by them? Why was it kept?"

" I have to tell you things that aren't normally passed onto mortals, things that are beyond your understanding. Look..." he said hurrying on when she scowled at him, "I believe the charm, as you call it, was handed down to one of your ancestors' millennia ago by a fallen angel. It has probably been in your family ever since. It cannot be destroyed or even discarded by a mortal. Ever! I think your parents realised its portent and that's why it was hidden away. As long as it wasn't passed on to the next generation it remained inert." He watched her face as she slowly took his explanation in. "Tell me something." He went on, "When you found it did you notice anything strange...anything inexplicable?"

Her eyes widened. "Oh my God yes... When I first held it, it seemed to give off heat. Only for a few seconds. I thought I had imagined it."

There was no hint of a smile from him now. He was deadly earnest. "You didn't imagine it. What you felt was its bonding with you. It had lost its way with the death of your Mother. Your father knew he couldn't destroy it. It was far too powerful, so he hid it. I should imagine he would have told you all about it eventually but he died suddenly didn't he?

Her eyes filled with tears. "He said he had things to tell me but he felt I was too young. He said that when I was eighteen he would tell me all about my mother but he died in a freakish accident when I was seventeen."

He clasped his hands together between his knees. He looked down at the sand beneath him. Amy felt that he was trying to decide how much more information she could process. He looked up into her face. He opened his mouth to say something but then decided against it

"I can see that there's a lot more that you're not telling me. There's something special about me isn't there?"

"Yes there is Amy. You are not like normal girls your age. You have Angel blood in you. I think that is what your father would have told you had he lived. You are what are known as a Nephilim. Part human and part Angel. You have certain divine powers. Does that make any sense to you?"

"I don't know what you mean. I'm just me. There's nothing special about me at all."

"Believe me Amy, you are special, you just don't know it yet." He smiled at her and this time there was such warmth in it that she bathed in its sweetness. What he was to say next however chilled her to the bone. "I don't believe your father's death was an accident. I think he was killed to keep him from revealing your hidden powers to you. For years he had kept you hidden from the forces of evil. By keeping you in the dark he believed that you were safe. He was right of course...while he was alive you were reasonably safe. Without him around the first thing you do is invoke evil beings to your presence by wearing that talisman."

As understanding of what he was telling her dawned on her, she grabbed the silver charm and yanked it over her head throwing it onto the sand away from her. She turned fearful eyes on him. "What can I do? You said humans couldn't destroy it."

He pushed himself up, strode over to where it lay and picked it up. "No but I can." With that he sprinted down the beach to the water's edge. She stood up quickly and watched him as he pulled his hand back and hurled the talisman and its chain over his head into the sea. If she hadn't seen it for herself she wouldn't have believed that anyone could have thrown something so far. As it sailed high over the waves they both heard an unholy almost animal scream that went on and on until it eventually hit the water way, way out, silencing it immediately. Malchediel stood for a few moments watching the sea. Amy, from her vantage point swore that the area of water where it had disappeared momentarily turned purple. She blinked and shading her eyes looked again...but all was normal. Malchediel turned and started walking back towards her. She hadn't, up until this point, been able to openly scrutinise him for fear that he would embarrass her by catching her staring. As he approached her from the shoreline there was nowhere else to look. She could watch him move towards her without having to look hastily away. His upper body was well-proportioned. His biceps were muscular but that alone wouldn't have accounted for the distance with which he threw the talisman, there had definitely been celestial forces at work there. His skin was unblemished and although he wasn't exactly tanned there was a somewhat golden glow about him. His hair also reflected the same golden glow, framing his face with soft rather windswept curls. He was still wearing the same cut-off cargo pants which were now liberally splashed with sea water and clinging to his calves. He reached up with one hand and casually brushed his hair from his face. "Did you hear that?" He called. "Now do you believe me? It was so full of malevolence, it was trying to work its way out of my grip."

She couldn't suppress a shudder at his words. "I can't understand how I didn't notice anything weird about it before now." She said as he came to stand in-front of her.

"That's because it didn't feel any threat from you before today. Rest assured it was sending messages back to its maker. Whoever was controlling it knew about your Guardians and eliminated them. Now that it's gone perhaps he will show himself."

"Oh my God! So that's not the end of it then?" she cried.

"I seriously doubt it, but we have the advantage now Amy. We know what we're dealing with."

"We do?"

He looked into her fearful eyes. "Only a Fallen Angel would have the power to control that kind of talisman. He will have to show himself now and this time he's not dealing with a benevolent Guardian...I fight back."

"So you will be staying with me now?"

"Of course." He answered surprised that she should feel the need to ask. "You are my mission." He gave a scornful laugh adding, "And I've never lost a battle yet."

She had the feeling that he was almost enjoying this assignment but that was fine because his air of confidence was infectious. She felt safer having him around.

Chapter Two

It took over half an hour for them to retrieve anything salvageable from her painting equipment. Her little stool was smashed beyond repair. One of the large boulders had landed squarely on-top of it. She couldn't even lift it but Malchediel rolled it off the splintered wood and carried it easily placing it under the overhang of the low cliff face. Together they collected everything up to carry back to the car. They worked mostly in silence as she checked what needed throwing away once they got back to Falmouth. The intention to spend the day painting on the beach had now gone and all she wanted was to get back home. The realisation that she had had a narrow escape unnerved her. Malchediel kept glancing at her but said nothing. After a little while she remembered his having climbed swiftly to the top of the overhang and looking over to him asked. "What were you looking for up there?"

He met her gaze, "I guessed it was no accident. I thought there may be some sort of evidence."

"And was there?"

"I couldn't see anything…"

She detected a 'but' and tilted her head indicating that she was waiting for him to go on. He straightened, holding her easel, "I thought I detected the odour of a demon."

"A what!" she exclaimed.

He drew in a deep breath and exhaled slowly before answering. "Fallen Angels rarely do their own dirty work. They will conjure up a low-life form…a demon for instance. They're dispensable and as long as their task is not too mentally demanding they are efficient workers."

She stood looking at him digesting what he had said. He returned her gaze standing still holding the easel in front of him. Slowly a smile twitched the corners of his mouth. Instantly she knew what he was finding so amusing. Her lips snapped to, quickly. "Okay, okay…so my mouth was open again. It's not surprising though, is it? You just keep hitting me with all this mumbo-jumbo. Until a few days ago my life was normal. Boring maybe, but there's a lot to be said for normality." He looked away still smiling to himself.

As they made their way back to the car she broached the subject of what he intended to do next. "I'm assuming that as I'm now your mission, you will want to stay with me."

"Do you find that objectionable?"

"It's preferable to an early demise I suppose."

He laughed as he held her hand to help her over a low stone wall marking the boundary of the beach. "I'm house-trained and I don't make much mess." She liked the way he was holding her hand and she was slow to disengage contact. "I just wonder what people will make of a strange man suddenly moving in with me."

"If the thought of gossip bothers you Amy, don't worry. Because of your Angel blood, you are able to see me. To other mortals I can make myself completely invisible. No-one need know anything about me." He let go of her hand waiting for her to open the boot of the car.

"You can do that?" she asked astounded. "You can make yourself invisible."

"Guardian Angels walk among mortals every day. Haven't you ever wondered why they are never seen?" She pressed her key fob opening the boot and waited until he had pushed the easel inside before answering. "Until today I hadn't given it much thought. I assumed Angels were just a myth. Now suddenly I'm having to re-think everything I have ever believed in. You talk about Fallen Angels and demons and Evil charms. This is a world I know nothing about." She bent forwards to place her painting table on-top of the easel, tucking the salvaged paints into the corner of the boot. Straightening up, she turned to him. "If I hadn't seen your wings for myself I wouldn't have believed it possible."

"Your father clearly felt that he was doing the right thing by not telling you about your heritage but by doing so he has left you unprepared to deal with what is happening to you now. There is so much you need to know. It's not going to be easy... What I will be telling you will shatter most of your pre-conceptions."

"After what has happened today my pre-conceptions are in tatters anyway." She pushed the boot closed and asked, "Will you be travelling back in the car or do you intend to fly back to Falmouth?"

The corner of his mouth quirked upwards, "As the wings are now packed away, could I hitch a lift with you?"

On the drive back to Falmouth Malchediel attempted to explain what the term Nephilim meant. As Amy had very little understanding of anything theological, he had to couch his explanations in the most basic terms. She listened to what he had to say occasionally asking questions when she didn't understand something. Her expression of shock when he defined the term Nephilim as the offspring of a mortal and an Angel quickly turned to disbelief. "But that can't be right." She insisted. "Both my parents were normal human beings. Neither of them were Angels." He hesitated before answering, forming his words so that she would understand. "Nephilim have been around for thousands of years. The first of them were a hybrid race of Mortal and Angelic beings. Over millennia providing that this strain of beings were not weakened by interbreeding with normal humans then their characteristics remained intact. It would seem Amy that all your ancestors were pure Nephilim. Any supernatural powers they possessed were passed down from generation to generation."

She drove on in silence digesting this information eventually asking, "Surely I would have noticed if I had any supernatural powers...or if my Dad could do strange things as well. There was never anything strange about him."

"I believe he supressed any Angelic qualities he may have possessed after the death of your mother in an attempt to protect you. It seems he mistakenly wanted you to grow up as an ordinary human being." He glanced sideways at her wondering how she would react to his almost critical view of her father's upbringing of her. When she said nothing he went on, "Look Amy...I know this is a lot for you to take in but you need to know about your background so that you can protect yourself in the future."

"Oh God...you're making it sound so scary. Up until today I was just a normal girl trying to get by. Now you pile all this on me...I don't know what to think." He took in the hunch of her shoulders, the tension in her arms as she gripped the steering wheel and he began to get an insight of the turmoil going on inside her. He laid his hand on hers and as she felt the calming strength flowing from him into her he said, "One thing you are not is 'normal' Amy. You have a direct unbroken line of Angelic force in you. Together we will find what your special powers are. You have already taken the first steps to accepting your new way of life. Over the next few days I'll tell you more about your heritage. You may even enjoy learning about it."

"I seriously doubt that." She murmured to herself. He heard the comment and smiled. Feeling that he had already overwhelmed her with revelations about her ancestry he changed the subject. "How long have you been selling your paintings?" She glanced sideways at him surprised at the change of topic. I've always enjoyed painting." She said turning her attention back to the road. "When Dad died I decided to make a career of it. He had left me enough money to set up my own little business. It didn't take long to build up a small collection of water colours and when the shop premises became available I negotiated a reasonable rent and opened up. Most of my sales are during the summer months and I make enough to last through the off-season. I also take on commissions to paint client's properties." She glanced quickly at him noting that he was watching her as she spoke. She felt her cheeks grow warm under his gaze. "Um...Can I ask you something?"

"Of course."

"Is it true that Angels are immortal?"

"Yes...that is to say that we don't grow old and eventually die like humans. We can be killed though but only by celestial forces." He watched as her brow furrowed in confusion.

"So...the Angel who first created the Nephi-thingy- line that has ended with me...could still be alive then?"

He grinned, "The word is Nephilim and yes, quite probably he is still around unless he was defeated in the war of the Fallen."

"Oh God, I'm going to wish I hadn't asked my next question. What on earth is the 'war of the Fallen?' "

"Have you heard of the term Fallen Angels?" he asked.

"Ahh...now that is something I remember from R.E at school. Lucifer took some of his fellow Angels and opposed God didn't he?"

He nodded. "Our Maker cast them out of Heaven for their disobedience. In anger they challenged those remaining loyal Angels and a vicious battle was fought culminating in Lucifer and his followers being banished to never-ending torment in what is now known as Hell. Many Angels were killed during this time...both the loyal and the Fallen."

She thought about this for a moment and then said, "I may regret asking this...Which side of the fence did my ancestor come from."

He hesitated and at once she knew the answer. "He was one of the Fallen, wasn't he?"

"It's clearly not what you wanted to hear Amy but only Fallen Angels mated with human women. They knew it was forbidden but after they had been cast out they seemed to enjoy breaking every rule in the book."

"So if my lineage is so tainted...how come you're here to protect me from whatever you feel is threatening me. And while we're on the subject why am I in danger anyway?"

He shifted in his seat so that he was looking at her profile. "Since you started wearing that talisman you have attracted the attention of one of the Fallen. Have you been aware of any little accidents or odd happenings recently?"

She thought for a moment, her brow furrowing again.

"What? Like that rock-fall today?"

"Yes...anything that seemed to threaten your well-being."

"Well...a few months ago I burnt myself. I was trying to light the fire and the match set fire to my fingers. I put it down to having spilled linseed oil over my hand earlier. A neighbour drove me to the casualty department." He watched as she tilted her hand to examine minor scarring down the inside of two fingers. She flicked a quick glance at him. "That surely was just a silly accident though?" She bit her bottom lip in consternation when he just shrugged his shoulders. "So if these little mishaps are down to some malevolent force...Why? What can be achieved by targeting me?"

"Whoever is doing this knows that we won't stand by and let it happen. We will always step in to prevent harm to humans. That's why two guardians were despatched for your protection. The fact that they have disappeared without trace gives credence to foul play at work here."

"Do you think they have been killed because of me?" she asked in a shocked voice.

"I don't know Amy but I intend to find out."

As Amy pulled up outside her cottage she turned to Malchediel. "This is where I live." She said. Now that they were outside her home she felt a little uneasy. It was clear that his intention was to stay with her. Had he been a normal human being this would not be happening. She had never lived with anyone other than her late father. Malchediel was an Angel and as such should be above any evil intent. He had said that he was only here to protect her and she believed him but as she glanced sideways at him she had to admit that he was one hell of an attractive guy and previous experience told her that men in blocking your Nephilimic capabilities as you were growing up. You were an unknown quantity to the Fallen until you found the talisman and started wearing it. Then they became aware of you and were able to track your movements. Unlike normal humans you do have the ability to see Angels and demons. After all you had no difficulty in seeing me when I came into your shop did you?"

She nodded remembering their first encounter. She was thoughtful for a moment mulling over what he had said, then she asked, "Can you help me to home-in on my supposed powers...you know, so that I can find out what they are?"

He regarded her solemnly before answering. "Okay, close your eyes Amy."

She did so and waited. "Now try to draw your conscious self, upwards."

She opened one eye fixing it on him. "I have no idea what you mean by that."

He exhaled noisily. "By all the saints!" he muttered.

"Sorry if this is an inconvenience." She retorted. They glared at one another before his lips twitched upwards.

"No it's me that should be sorry. Raguel owes me big time for this. From Warrior to teacher...I must have really annoyed him in the past." He smiled at her and she relaxed. "Right, let's try something a little different." He added. He put his plate down and turned to her. "Do you know what an aura is?" he asked.

Isn't it some sort of coloured glow around a person's body?" she answered.

Still smiling, his eyes moved upwards looking above her head. "Yes, and yours is a very soft green aura edged with silver." He focused back on her face, "very pretty." He added. "Now concentrate...look slightly above my head. Empty your mind of any thoughts...relax...what do you see?"She did exactly what he instructed and stared above his head. A minute went by. Eventually her eyes dropped back to his face. "Nothing." She said with disappointment.

"Hang on, I've had a thought." He said suddenly, "Do you remember those weird pictures that were fashionable on Earth a couple of decades ago. They looked like optical patterns when you first looked at them…"

"Yes, I know what you mean. You had to look through them to see a hidden picture. Is that what you want me to try?"

He nodded. She looked above his head once more but this time instead of focussing on the wall behind him she picked up on one small point and stared at it remembering how she had viewed all those odd patterns in the past. The seconds ticked by and all at once she cried, "Got it, I've got it. It's Blue…Oh God it's beautiful. It's the most startling blue I've ever seen."

"It's aquamarine actually." He said quietly. "Now concentrate on that blue okay?"

She nodded.

"Slowly close your eyes."

"But it will disappear."

"Try it."

She hesitated for a moment then slowly closed her eyes. "Oh Mal, I can still see it." She breathed in astonishment. "I can still see it with my eyes closed."

"That's because you're a Nephilim Amy. Now you're getting the hang of it."

Her eyelids flickered open and her eyes locked on his and she had the strangest feeling. He was watching her, a slight smile on his lips. She looked at those lips and wondered what it might be like to kiss them. She mentally shook herself. What was she thinking, he was an Angel. Weren't they made of all things good…above such things as sexual desire? Would he be horrified if he knew what she was thinking? *Stop looking at his lips for heaven's sake.* She raised her eyes to his…he was still watching her and she quickly looked away in confusion. He seemed not to notice anything amiss or if he did he said nothing. "Have you had enough to eat?" she asked hastily. He pushed himself back on the sofa lifting one leg so that his ankle rested loosely across his knee. She found his mannerisms disconcerting. He didn't act like the archetypal Angel. Weren't they supposed to wander, eyes downcast, hands held in perpetual prayer exuding constant goodness. Perhaps she had been sent the one and only sexy Angel that Heaven had on its books. She was bought back to herself by his voice, "Yes thank you Amy. The honey was every bit as delicious as I remember."

"Were you serious when you said that it had been about two hundred years since you had eaten it last?"

"Give or take a decade or two, yes."

"Given our normal lifespan here on Earth that sounds so bizarre. Um...can I ask you a personal question?"

"You want to know how old I am." She felt her face colouring but she nodded.

"Let's just say I'm a lot older than you." He wasn't going to get away with that for an answer.

"Are we talking Millennia here?" she pursued. He regarded her for a moment before answering softly, "Yes."

The silence between them lengthened as she thought about that.

"Come on Amy." He said breaking into her thoughts, "Let's unload the car shall we?"

Together they carried everything back into the cottage. She was relieved to find that on inspection her water colour paints weren't badly damaged and once the sand had been cleaned off them she packed them away. Likewise the easel was intact. The little table was damaged beyond repair but she knew that there was another similar stool at the shop that could be requisitioned in its place. "You had barely started your painting when the rock fall occurred." He said as she was inspecting her brushes, "Do you intend to go back there to finish it off?"

"I will if you come with me...I wouldn't fancy going back there alone after what you've told me." She packed the brushes away with the paints before asking, "Are you certain that it wasn't an accident?"

"Absolutely, it definitely wasn't an accident Amy. Trust me. Something is going on here. Two things could happen now. Either whoever is behind this will give up knowing that I'm now here to protect you, or…they will show their face and I will do whatever I have to."

She closed her box of paints and looked up at his face, "Thank you for being there today." She gave a nervous little laugh, "I'm still coming to terms with everything that's happened…Not just the idea that someone or something is trying to hurt me but the whole concept of the Angel thing. I have to revise all that I've ever believed in. It's not easy for someone who has never been religiously inclined in the past."

He had been standing hands in his pockets watching her sorting through her equipment. Now he pushed one of the sofa cushions aside and sat down next to her. "Religion means different things to different people. It's just a word Amy. You believe that there is good and evil in the world don't you?"

"Of course."

"Then you have the cornerstone of what religion is about. There is a constant battle between good and evil. Hopefully the good deeds will always outweigh the bad. You don't have to be a God-botherer to do the right thing." He grinned.

"You really are not what I expected an Angel to be like." She giggled. "How on earth would you know a term like that?"

"We Heavenly beings like to keep abreast of the times you know. It's been a while since we dropped 'thee, thy and thine' from our vocabulary."

"A twenty first century Angel…and one that knows computing terms too, that's quite a novelty."

"We wouldn't be much use to mankind if we still lived in the times of Sodom and Gomorrah would we?"

"And I suppose you remember those two unholy towns?"

He gave a theatrical shudder, "Ugh, you wouldn't take your mother there I can tell you."

She shook her head still smiling. "Did you have one...a mother?"

"It was just a figure of speech." He glanced up at the window. "It's too nice to be indoors, shall we go for a walk. I would like to familiarise myself with the area around here." It was a sudden change of subject and she wondered if he preferred not to talk about himself. There must be quite a history to him; after all he had lived for a long, long time.

"Okay." She said reaching for her cardigan.

Once outside, her spirits lifted. It was mid-afternoon. The sun was shining, the few clouds that there were, were high and wispy. Amy shielded her eyes and looked up watching the vapour trail slowly trace the passage of a jet liner. It was so high that there was no sound from it and the plane itself was only visible as a shining speck reflecting the sunlight. She was aware that Malchediel was watching her and she thrust her hands in the pockets of her jeans and started walking down the lane away from the cottage. Within a couple of strides he had caught up with her and fell into step. Without looking at him she asked, "You know we were talking earlier about the time when some of the Angels rebelled and were banished from Heaven?"

"Uh-hu..." he answered wondering what was coming next.

"Well...God is supposed to be all-forgiving and kind but He was determined to punish them. No second chances. Don't you think it was a little bit severe?"

He raised one perfectly shaped eyebrow considering her question. She didn't know it but their fall from grace had had a profound effect on him at the time. No-one then could have foreseen the catastrophic consequences of what started as an insubstantial difference of opinion. Indeed even Malchediel himself had become embroiled in the initial disputes over the limits of the Angel's powers. Only when he could see that neither side was going to give way did he make the decision to 'toe the line' and throw in his lot with the Maker and by the skin of his teeth managed to keep his place within the realm of Heaven when many of his comrades were banished. He realised that he had made the right decision but it had been a close call and Raguel for one had never let him forget how close he had come to joining the Fallen. He cleared his throat, "God expects total obedience from us. His benevolence has its limits and he certainly won't tolerate any lack of discipline. He has much more toleration for you mortals. You are his children and as such he almost expects you to misbehave from time to time. As a much older race we are expected to have outgrown such rebellious ways."

She pondered his answer as they walked on a little way. Giving him a sideways glance she eventually asked, "Have you never wanted to do something bad?" She saw him start to smirk.

"Ohh Amy what a question." Was all he said. She chuckled but let the matter drop. Had she have known about his sympathies during the war of the Fallen and how close he himself had come to joining their ranks she would have gleaned a better insight into his less than Angelic countenance. As it was she was finding his slightly irreverent attitude growing on her. Although she had been annoyed when he had found it amusing that she had bumped her head when they had first met, she now revised that earlier opinion of him. He hadn't intended his off-the-cuff comment to be hurtful. She felt that he hadn't been laughing at her, he had been laughing with her. As they walked on he asked her about her life since the death of her father and she found herself opening up to him, something that she hadn't done with anyone else before. He learned that following her father's accident she had completed her 'A' levels at school and then decided to invest the small bequest from him in opening the little shop off the High Street and set up as an artist. Before she had a chance to enquire where he had decided to hang the painting that he had purchased he asked her what she did for recreation when she wasn't working.

"I keep in touch with friends from school." She said. "Most of them went on to University or college so I don't see them until holiday time. That's when we all get together and go to clubs or the cinema. If money is tight we just hang out in bars or cafes."

"Do you have a boyfriend?" he asked.

"That's a personal question. Is it relevant to what-ever is going on here?" She asked with a grin. As they had been walking along the quiet lane bordered by high hedges he had been kicking a small stone, catching up with it and kicking it again. Now he stopped, the stone near the toe of his shoe. He bought his leg back and kicked again sending the stone skittering several yards ahead to be lost in the overgrown verge. Turning to her he hesitated before answering. "I was just wondering if there was someone close to you that you would want to discuss the reason for my being here "

"Would you prefer that no-one knew who...or what you are?"

He gave a humourless snort. "Do you really think anyone would believe you if you told them you have an Angel protecting you?"

"There is that, unless you were to display those wings of yours. Anyway I thought you could make yourself invisible to ordinary mortals."

"That's no problem for me but you could find it difficult having me around trying to pretend I'm not there when you're with someone else."

"Well you don't have to worry, there isn't a boyfriend on the scene and as you said yourself who would believe me anyway if I told them about you?" He smiled at her answer as they walked on a little way in silence. "What do you think will happen next?" she asked.

"That I don't know Amy. I am certain that there is a Fallen Angel behind this. Why you have been targeted ...again I don't know. One thing is certain though. He knows I am here. The Fallen are not cowards...he will show himself." He saw how she struggled with this news and he stopped again and turned placing both of his hands on her shoulders. She looked up into his face. He smiled slowly giving her shoulders an affectionate squeeze. "Have a little faith in me Amy. I won't let anything happen to you."

Later that evening following a supper of tomato soup and crackers they sat and talked. He had said that he had no need of food so she assumed that he joined her merely to be sociable. She learned that if he did eat at all, it was as a vegetarian. He said that the thought of eating something that had once been alive was repugnant to him and although she did eat meat she could understand his feelings on the matter. She kept him talking until quite late putting off the inevitable moment when she knew she would have to go to bed. By midnight she was beginning to stifle a few yawns.

"You're tired Amy. Why don't you go to bed? I'll check down here, make sure everything is secure then I'll come up."

She had never got herself ready for bed so quickly. By the time he came up to her room she was already in bed, the duvet up to her chin, her hands gripping the edges tightly. She watched him come into the room. By the light of her bedside lamp she could see him stride across the room to the window. He loosened the catch but left it closed. Without turning to her he said quietly, "We'll hear if anything tries to get in. If it's a demon it will have to use the window. Unlike us they can't move through walls."   At his words realisation hit her like a sledgehammer.

"That's how you got into the shop without me hearing you last week. You didn't use the door."

"I knew you'd eventually get it." He said tilting the blinds so they were partially open. "Turn off the lamp Amy." She did as he asked and after a few seconds her eyes grew accustomed to the pale silvery moonlight cutting slivers through the blinds. He glanced across at her and as she watched he stripped off his shirt laying it across the back of the little armchair that stood against the wall. "What are you doing?" she whispered. She couldn't see his face clearly but she knew he was smiling as he answered. "If anything happens tonight I may need to use my wings...it's a bit difficult trying to unfurl them through clothing. What were you thinking Amy? That I was going to strip off for you?"   She felt her face burning at his words and was glad that it was dark in the room.

"In your dreams Angel." She hissed. He laughed softly settling himself in the armchair. Silence descended on the room. After a few minutes he heard her yawn again, the rustle of the duvet as she turned on her side and then the steady breathing as she slipped into sleep. She awoke with a start. It was dark in the room. There was no longer any moonlight shining across the carpet. She turned her head towards the clock. Five thirty.

"Mal?" she whispered.

"I'm here." Came his voice from across the room.

"Nothing happened?" she asked.

"Nope."

"Did you sleep at all?" she asked quietly.

"I couldn't with all your snoring."

"I do not snore!"

"Alright...heavy breathing then."

"Do you never let up? It's barely dawn and you're already full on with the sarcasm."

He laughed. "Alright you don't snore...you do mutter a little in your sleep though."

She pushed herself up on her elbows looking towards the armchair although she couldn't see him. "Now I know that's the truth. Dad said I sometimes talked in my sleep."

He heard the wistfulness in her voice. "You still miss him?"

She lay back down. "Hmm." She acknowledged. After a pause she asked, "Why do you think nothing happened?" She heard the chair creak as he got up. He wandered over to the window and opened the blinds fully. She saw the muted red dawn breaking beyond the glass, his torso bathed in its glow. He leaned forward resting his palms on the window sill as he peered out over the surrounding fields. "He's either planning his next move or he's just toying with us. My guess is the latter." He turned towards the bed. "But are we unnerved Amy?" he said brightly.

"Too bloody right we are!"   "

Ohhh… Amy, Amy, I'm upset by your lack of faith in me." He said feigning a look of deep hurt.

"This is like a game to you isn't it?" She said crossly pushing herself back up into a sitting position. He came and sat down on the edge of the bed and she was acutely aware of the warmth coming from his upper body. "Would you rather that I was nervous and exuding anxiety?"

"No of course not…but perhaps a little more sobriety would help. This is scary."

He held her gaze for a moment. "When the time comes there will be no wise cracks, until then this is the way I am." He clicked his tongue a couple of times and gave her a cheeky wink. Then standing up he stretched his arms above his head saying, "Fancy a cup of tea?"

After breakfast he asked her if she wanted to go back to Gunwalloe to carry on with her painting but when faced with the prospect of seeing where she had narrowly escaped injury she felt that it was too soon. "I think I would rather leave it a while longer before I venture back there." She said. "I don't usually open the shop on Monday or Tuesday but there is work I can carry on with there."

Malchediel sat back tilting the back legs of the kitchen chair precariously. "Okay…the shop it is then." He didn't add that wherever she was she was now vulnerable. The shop was no safer than the beach. "I could do with buying some more clothes anyway so a trip into Falmouth suits me." He said instead.

"That reminds me." She said "I was going to ask you about how you paid for your painting. Do Angels carry money?" He let the chair fall back onto all four legs, a smile spreading across his face. "Ahh…" he said, "I have a confession to make about that."

Before he could explain, Amy interrupted. "Well as we're in the mood for confessions…I have one of my own to make." He waited. "You know I said the price of the painting was one hundred and twenty five pounds."

He gave a little nod.

"Well it was only worth fifty pounds really."

He gave her a stern look.

"Well…you annoyed me… the way you thought banging my head was funny…on the spur of the moment I wanted to get my own back. I didn't think for one minute you would pay it."

"Ohh Amy…that wasn't a very nice thing to do. Was it?"

"Well," she said feeling very embarrassed, "I was annoyed with you at the time." She looked across the table at him. "I did feel guilty after you left. How about I refund the extra? Will that earn your forgiveness?" she wheedled.

"I suppose it will go some way to earning your redemption." He said finally.
She laughed at his failed attempt to keep a straight face. "Okay, that's my confession, what's yours?"

"You'll find out when we get to the shop." Was all he said.

On the drive into Falmouth she badgered him with questions about what her 'special powers' could possibly be.

"I wish I could tell you Amy. I have no more idea about them than you."

"But you know all about Nephilim. You must have some inkling about what other half angels can do."

"It can be anything…erm…mind reading or being able to

you want me to call round tonight? I'll ask my Dad for some more background information on your Mum." To Malchediel he added, "It may throw some light on what's been happening to Amy lately."

After Stephen had left, Amy sat down on the counter top. Malchediel stood facing her, hands in his back pockets. "So you had no idea that your friend was a Nephilim too?"

"There must be something in an Angelic background that makes us all so secretive." she replied.

He gave the briefest of smiles at her comment adding,

"A lot of things are falling into place now though. It is common knowledge that the Nephilim were split in their allegiance to the Angels after the fall. All were the offspring of the Fallen but many despised what they had become after they had been cast down. In the beginning many formed themselves into fighting units working along-side Warrior Angels when needed. Eventually because of their limited angelic powers most Angels preferred to fight alone. There were great differences of opinion between us so from then on the Nephilim fighters preferred to work alone also." He paused before adding, " Nephilim fighters were often killed during these skirmishes." He took in her pinched face. "I think your mind must be in melt down by now." He said trying to lighten the mood. Then with a swift change of subject he asked, "Do you remember asking me whether Angels carried money and I said I had a confession to make?"

Her worried expression changed to one of interest, "Go on." She invited.

"Check under your work-bench." He said with a smile. She gave him a bewildered look before bending down to peer beneath the bench. There leaning against one of the stout wooden legs was a brown paper parcel. Pulling it out she looked up at him. "Is this the Gunwalloe that you bought?"

"It is. That's my confession. I didn't buy it."

"I don't understand." She said lifting up the package and placing it on the bench. "You paid for it. I saw you leave with it. What is it doing back here?" She was confused. "I saw you walk out of the shop with it. You paid for it in cash. I have the money in my bag. I was going to bank it today." She reached for her handbag as a slow smile spread across his face. Opening her purse she pulled out the notes. "Twenty, forty, sixty, seventy, eighty, ninety, one hundred." She counted, before searching all the other compartments. Even counting out the coins she only totalled one hundred and eight pounds and a few odd pennies. "How did you do that? I counted out the cash when you paid me. I remembered putting it in my purse."

"You think you did. I put that thought there. I needed an excuse to meet you Amy. What better way than to come into your shop as a customer."

"What a sneaky way to go about it, making me believe that you bought a painting from me. Hardly the behaviour of an Angel is it?" she said but she was finding it difficult not to smile at his audacity.

"And this from someone who inflated the price by over one hundred per cent. I don't think you are in a position to preach morals Amy. Anyway the painting never left your possession so no crime was committed."

"Fair enough I'll give you this one misdemeanour." She laughed as she put the money back in her purse. He was glad that she was now in a happier mood. He let his eyes linger on her smiling face as she started to unwrap the Gunwalloe painting. He realised with not a little surprise that he was warming to the task that he had at first found so demeaning to his rank.

At lunchtime Stephen called back to Amy's shop. He said that he had spoken to his father by phone and that he had suggested that if Amy was agreeable to it, he would accompany Stephen to her house later that evening to discuss with her and Malchediel everything he knew about her mother's past. At last she would find out what sort of life her mother had been leading prior to her death. Both she and Malchediel agreed to the meeting. After arranging to be at her cottage at around eight o'clock Stephen left but not before asking Amy how she was getting on having an Angel around. They were standing in the doorway of the shop and were out of range of Mal's hearing. Glancing quickly behind her to make sure they couldn't be overheard, Amy told him that he was nothing like what she had expected an Angel to be, had she have believed in their existence in the first place, but under the circumstances she was glad he was around.

After lunch Malchediel asked if there was anywhere where he could purchase more clothing.

"So Angels do carry cash then?" She commented.

"Not usually... but I do have one of these." He said fishing a piece of black plastic from the back pocket of his cargo pants. It was the same size and shape as a normal bank smart card but it was completely blank on both sides. "Don't tell me." She said, "You lot have your own bank account."

"You're catching on." There was just the hint of condescension in his voice. "I never leave home without it."

"Okay, let's do some retail therapy." She said rolling her eyes as she lifted her jacket from the coat hook. She had known him for less than a week but she had already accepted that there was little he couldn't achieve using Celestial forces so when he withdrew two hundred pounds from a bank cash point using what appeared to be a totally blank card, she wasn't surprised. They spent the next hour adding to his meagre wardrobe of tee shirt and cargo pants and later back at her little shop she confessed that in jeans a dark blue sweater he had never looked less like an Angel. Adjusting the belt at his waist he remarked, "Like I said before, we move with the times. It would draw attention to me if I wandered around Falmouth in biblical robes wouldn't it?" She had to agree that apart from his amazing Californian surfer looks there was nothing remotely holy about him. Whilst eating a late lunch of salad rolls purchased from the bakery Amy questioned him about his life as a warrior Angel. She was sitting on the counter, he opposite her on the work bench. He was evasive when she asked about Heaven itself giving no details of what his life there was like. He spoke freely however about his work defending the mortals of planet Earth. She learned that he worked in a team with three other Angels. They had been together for several centuries and had established a working ethos of trust and close comradeship.

"Have you ever done anything like this before?" she asked, "Working alone without anyone watching your back?"

He told her that this was the first ever solo mission that he had undertaken. "The team was one member down once." He added, "When Nemamiah lost part of a wing to a particularly aggressive goblin. That put him out of action for some time. We could have recruited a temporary fourth Angel during this time but we managed without. It's never the same working with someone new. We knew each other's ways so well…some-one new would have been a hindrance rather than a help so we managed, just the three of us until Nem had recovered." He brushed crumbs from the front of his sweater before unscrewing the cap from a bottle of water and taking a deep drink. She watched - her lunch momentarily forgotten as the muscles in his neck flexed. She found the simple gesture of him drinking strangely attractive almost erotic and she looked away quickly before he noticed her staring at him. She cleared her throat, "So… did Nemamiah's wing eventually grow back?" she asked.

"Eventually…yes with Raphael's ministrations he was soon as good as new."

"Have you ever been injured during one of your battles?"

"Nothing serious. The odd cut, an occasional infected bite. The worst I ever encountered was acid burns from the saliva of a Gunneraptor." He pushed the sleeve of his sweater up exposing dark scarring on the inner side of his wrist.

"I'm not even going to ask what on earth a Gunneraptor is, but where did that happen?"

His eyes narrowed as he thought back to the time that he was talking about. "I think that was in Mongolia." He closed his eyes briefly before confirming, "No it was China back in the twelfth century. I haven't seen one for a long time now. I think they were so unpredictable that even the warlocks who conjured them up couldn't control them so they were abandoned to their fate in hell."

She started to smile and he asked, "What?"

"You live in another world. All this is like something from a Sci-fi comic."

"It's actually your world we're talking about Amy. It's just that most mortals don't know what's going on around them." She sobered at his words and suddenly her appetite had gone. She wrapped up the remains of her lunch and dropped it in the bin. The room had gone silent, neither of them elaborating on what they were thinking. Amy slid off the counter and turning her back to him opened her own bottled water. She raised it but before taking a drink she asked quietly, "Do you think my Mum would have known all about this sort of thing...the demons and goblins and suchlike?" He hesitated before answering her. "If she was part of a Nephilim active fighting force, then I'm sure she would have been well aware of these creatures Amy." She didn't answer but he saw her nod her head in acceptance of this information.

They spent the rest of the afternoon stretching canvas over wooden frames building up a mixed selection of canvases for future use. Later with Mal's help Amy re-arranged the hung paintings so that the Gunwalloe watercolour could be re-hung on the back wall.

On the drive back to the cottage that evening Malchediel asked Amy what she knew about Stephen's family. She told him that she had met his parents only occasionally when she and Stephen had been at school together. Her own father had shunned socialising so the only contact she had had with them was at parents evening once a year. They had seemed friendly but she had put that down to the fact that Stephen had always 'had a thing' for her. At this Malchediel flicked a quick glance at her profile as she drove. She didn't meet his gaze but he thought he detected a pink blush creep up her neck. Deciding not to pursue this topic he gave voice to his thoughts, "Your father was clearly aware that they were Nephilim. Stephen said that he told them you weren't to be told about your background. It will be interesting to hear what they have to say this evening."

Amy made a supper of pasta, flavoured with a tomato and mushroom sauce. As a courtesy to Mal she too had for the time being adopted a vegetarian diet. With the dishes finally cleared away the two of them settled down to await the arrival of Stephen and his father. Malchediel had told her over supper that he enjoyed wine occasionally when working on Earth and they sat in companionable comfort sharing a bottle of Muscadet together. "Are you intending to repeat last night's exercise?" she asked leaning over to close the blinds at the living room window against the darkness outside. "Yes," he answered swallowing the wine he was savouring, "And every evening from now on until something happens."

She turned on a small table lamp beside the sofa casting a warm glow across Malchediel's face. "These Nephilim must be a very secretive bunch. How on Earth can they exist alongside normal human beings without attracting attention to themselves?"

"You speak of them as if they are an alien race Amy. Don't forget you are one of them and a pure bred at that." He said with amusement in his voice. "Which reminds me that we need to try to unravel what powers you possess?"

"Well...good luck with that. I think you may be sadly disappointed on that score."

"Come and sit down beside me I want to try something." He suggested patting the sofa next to him. As she did so he turned sideways so that they were facing one another.

He looked into her eyes saying, "Just relax and listen to me."

She nodded and waited.

"What is your full name?" He asked.

She frowned. That wasn't what she was expecting. "Well?" he said.

She shrugged slightly, "Amy Elizabeth Bernstein."

"How old are you Amy?"

"Nineteen... almost twenty."

"What is your favourite colour?"

Her brows drew together. "What are you trying to do?" she asked impatience beginning to show.

He sighed. "Just answer the questions Amy and stop getting exasperated."

She pursed her lips. "Purple I suppose."

"And what is your favourite season?"

"Spring...I like spring the best." She answered without hesitation.

Why Spring? He sent the thought to her.

"I suppose because it's the start of a new year. Baby lambs...spring flowers...April showers."

He said nothing, he just looked at her.

"What?" she said perplexed.

I didn't speak Amy. He pushed the thought at her.

Suddenly she realised what he meant. "Oh my God! Oh my God! But I heard you. I heard you in my head. It was so clear."

He smiled at her reaction. "I had a feeling that you may be telepathic."

Her eyes were round with wonder. "Is it just with you that I can do that?"

"I shouldn't think so. When I said telepathic I don't think you will be able to read people's thoughts unbidden. It's not uncommon for Nephilim to receive projected thoughts. Messages sent by thought rather than by the spoken word."

"Can you do that?" she asked.

"Try me." He said, a knowing smile lifting the corners of his mouth. "Send me a message."

She closed her eyes sending out a question to him. He lifted his glass to her. "Yes please."

She clapped her hands gleefully before topping up his glass.

Just after eight o'clock Stephen and his father pulled up outside the cottage. Amy found that as she was welcoming them into her home for the first time she was feeling quite nervous. She knew that tonight she was going to learn an awful lot about her late mother's activities and she wasn't altogether sure how she was going to react to these revelations. Stephen smiled warmly at her and unlike his father who seated himself in the armchair opposite her; he sat right next to her. Malchediel took the other chair facing Alex Goodrich, who was the first to speak addressing himself to Malchediel. "Erm…You will have to forgive me if I appear nervous…I've never been in the presence of an Angel before…not even sure how I should be addressing you."

"Mal is fine. Please be at ease we're all here to try to help Amy adjust to her new role as one of the Nephilim. I believe you were aware of her background which is more than can be said of Amy herself." He turned a warm smile on her as he spoke but all she could think of was Stephen's thigh pressed against her own.

Alex cleared his throat nervously, "Stephen tells me that you would like me to fill you in on all I remember of Melissa." Looking towards Amy he added, "I remember your mother so very well my dear." Amy acknowledged his comment with a smile taking the opportunity to unobtrusively re-settle herself so that there was now an inch or two space between her and Stephen.

"Within the Nephilim circle Melissa was well known." He went on. "I would be surprised if her name wasn't known across Europe. She was a skilled fighter despatching many a demon or indeed any type of malignant spirit. She was the scourge of the Fallen, whenever there was a sighting she was the first to be called upon. Not surprising really," He said looking over at Malchediel, "She was a Monkshood before she became a Bernstein." Malchediel nodded acknowledging the comment.

"A Monkshood?" queried Amy, "Is that significant in some-way?"

As Alex Goodrich emitted a brief sharp laugh, Malchediel explained, "For generations the Monkshoods were famous soldiers in the relentless battle against evil. They were hated by the Fallen for their prowess at foiling any plans of theirs to create havoc on Earth. I didn't know that she was part of that family." He added to Alex.

Stephen's father nodded, "She knew that she was a marked woman. There couldn't have been a Fallen Angel that didn't want her dead. I didn't agree with your father for keeping you in the dark about your maternal heritage Amy," he said turning his attention back to her, "But I could understand it. He must have been terrified for your safety after she was killed." He hesitated before going on with his reminisces. "I remember when he came to see me and my wife a few weeks after your mother's funeral. He was a broken man my dear. I truly believe that it was only his love for you that kept him from attempting to follow your mother into the hereafter. He missed her so much...he was never a fighter you see Amy. He was a gentle man who lived for his family and now you were all that he had left. He made us promise never to divulge your mother's background to you. He wanted to keep you safe and who could blame him for that?"

"So you agreed to his request and Amy was allowed to grow up ignorant of her Nephilim legacy." Malchediel put in.

"What else could we do? In the event it proved the right thing to do. There never seemed to be any risk to Amy as she grew up into a very charming young lady." He smiled warmly at her and she became aware once again of Stephen's thigh pressing closely against hers. She looked quickly to Malchediel catching his smirk of amusement at Alex's comment before his face took on a mask of cool detachment.

Is it so funny that someone finds me charming? She sent a thought to him, only to receive a barely noticeable lift of one eyebrow. Alex's voice drew them back. "I think Amy, that had your mother lived your upbringing would have been completely different. As Malchediel said, for generations the Monkshoods were renowned for taking up arms whenever there was a need. There is a well- known legend back in the early seventeenth century when several members of three families in a small area of Suffolk mysteriously disappeared over a period of a few months. They were Nephilim. The Monkshoods were alerted and it was discovered that one by one they had been enticed to the home of a local magistrate under the pretext of investigating legal documents relating to their properties. Once there, they had been murdered and their bodies buried in woodland nearby. Of course the magistrate was above suspicion so no legal action could be taken. Murdoch Monkshood ended his murderous campaign one night and the magistrate was never seen again. There were never any more Nephilim disappearances after that. Legend has it that letters were found by Murdoch at the Magistrates home listing the names of members of all three families. Those that had already disappeared had been crossed through. Pretty condemning evidence it seemed. All the letters had been signed A. Mammon."

Amy glanced quickly at Malchediel as he exhaled sharply at hearing the name. "Does that name mean anything to you?" she asked.

"It does." He said, "I imagine you know the name also." He shot at Alex who nodded his assent. He sighed before informing Amy, "Mammon was one of the first Angels to fall. He was a close friend of Lucifer. It's a name I haven't heard for a very long time." He leaned back in the armchair stretching his legs out in-front of him for a moment lost in some distant memory- no doubt Amy thought- recalling the one time Angel Mammon now residing somewhere outside the Celestial realm that was once his home. "Surely that was just a legend Mister Goodrich?" Amy suggested.

He shrugged, "Who knows for certain Amy dear. It's a story well known in Nephilim circles that's all I know." Amy felt a chill pass down her spine at the story of a one- time ancestor of her maternal family taking revenge for the deaths of other Nephilim almost four hundred years ago. It seemed to her that these people were a law unto themselves living and operating outside of the legal system of the land and her mother had been one of them…she herself was one of them. Alex's voice bought her out of her reverie. "Stephen has explained to me the reason for your being here. " He directed at Malchediel, "May I ask what it is you intend to do to protect Amy?"

Malchediel leaned forward rubbing his hands slowly backward and forwards along his thighs, "I shall be staying here with Amy until whatever is targeting her makes another move. I need to find out who is behind this. I also want to find out what has happened to the two guardians who were sent before me. I have never heard of guardian Angels just disappearing before. It has to be the work of the Fallen…no mortal being would have the power to make that happen."

"Is there anything we can do to assist?" Stephen asked. Malchediel turned what could only be described as a look of distain towards him, "I think I have it covered." He said.

Amy felt inwardly for Stephen but said nothing fearing to make the situation even more embarrassing for him. Malchediel went on, "I think we can assume from what we now know that Amy's familial background is the key to what has been going on here. I still intend to flush out the one responsible. It has to be one of the Fallen Angels…only they use the type of demon that I have so far detected."

"So…if and when you come face to face with who-ever it is; what will you do?" Amy asked.

the creature, his own hands with fingers curled inviting it closer. The creature shook its head in aggravation flecks of drool flying left and right. Again Malchediel motioned for it to step forward…he was treating this like a game. Amy began to realise that he was enjoying it. *Be careful.* She sent the thought to him. The dwarf-like thing hadn't moved and Malchediel took the opportunity to glance quickly up at the window flashing a wicked smile in her direction. It was the diversion the creature needed. With astonishing speed for its build it lunged at Malchediel braying with its mouth wide, its claws extended. Amy screamed a warning her hands braced against the glass. The creature was fast but Mal was faster. He caught it by the throat, one hand gripping tightly cutting off its airway. Holding it above the ground he bought its face in line with his own and appeared to be looking into its eyes and that's how they stayed for several seconds eye to eye but far enough away for its teeth and claws to do no damage. It seemed as though Mal was speaking to it but from where she stood she could hear nothing. The creature struggled but it was locked in Mal's vice-like grip. Without warning it abruptly ceased its thrashing movements and became limp. *Be careful…it could be a trick;* she pushed into Mal's head. Without turning to her he shook his head letting the creature drop to the ground where like the first one it fragmented into hundreds of pieces before disappearing completely. As she watched Malchediel bent down to rub his hands into the grass. She guessed touching the creature had been to say the least unpleasant. He slowly stood up and turned back towards the cottage. With two strong beats of his wings he rose up towards the window where she stood. Within a moment he had materialised back into the room and stood facing her. Without saying a word he drew his shoulders back and retracted his wings never once taking his eyes from her face. Now that he was back in the room with her, the enormity of what she had just witnessed took a hold and she began to shake. "Oh God Mal…Oh God…I thought they were going to kill you." Tears welled up in her eyes and before her legs gave way he was holding her, his mouth against her forehead. "It will take more than a couple of goblins to kill me Amy." She rested against his chest acutely aware of the warmth of his skin and the smell of him... a fragrance she couldn't pin down but found immensely pleasant. His arms felt strong and safe and she was happy to stay just where she was. "You're getting quite good at thought transference." He murmured. She could feel his lips moving against her skin and she leaned even closer into him.

"You heard me?" she whispered.

"Loud and clear. Thanks for the warning. I knew that there were two of them but I wasn't aware the second one was so close."

"What the hell were they? They were hideous." She felt his body shake with silent laughter.

"You're right they wouldn't win any beauty contests would they? They were just Goblins...malformed low intelligent wretches. If a Fallen Angel sent them I guess he's toying with us."

She pulled her head back to look up at him, "Why do you say that?"

"Because they pose little threat to a Warrior Angel. You saw how quickly they gave up. That's why I sent a message back to their perpetrator."

She didn't understand what he was saying. "What do you mean? How could you send a message. It died in your hands. It <u>did</u> die didn't it? When it disappeared I mean."

"Oh yes." He agreed, "They're both dead now. I killed the first one but the second must have been despatched by its controller. I was hoping to interrogate it first but no matter... before it disappeared I sent a message back through its eyes. The eyes act like a camera to its controller. Whoever is behind this would have been able to see and hear me. I've now introduced myself so-to-speak. He or she knows I'm on to them." A smile slowly spread across his face, "What happens next will be interesting."

"So you don't think you've scared off whoever is behind

all of this then?"

"Ohh I hope not. It's getting interesting now." He said clicking his tongue and winking at her in the most devilish way. As she looked at him incredulity plainly showing on her face he grinned then he sniffed the air and raising his hand to his face sniffed at it, "By all the saints!" he exclaimed, "They certainly stink. Can I use your shower?"

He returned to the room twenty minutes later wearing a different pair of jeans. His feet were bare as was his torso but he lifted one of his tee-shirts from Amy's top drawer. Pulling it over his head carefully avoiding his towel-dried hair he turned to her. She was sitting up in bed, her hands clasped around her raised knees. "I thought you weren't able to unfurl your wings if you were wearing a shirt." She said.

"There won't be any more nocturnal visits for a while. There's too much for our assailant to think through."

"I hope you're right." She answered resting her chin on her knees but keeping her eyes on him. "You're probably used to brawling with monsters in the dead of night but I was absolutely terrified watching you from up here."

"Brawling makes me sound like an out-of-control hooligan." He said with some amusement in his voice, "But you're right I am used to handling this kind of creature. I'm not human Amy. They aren't much of a risk to me. If I get injured I can recover quickly unlike you mortals. That's why we are sent to sort out these mystical beings." He ran his fingers through his blonde curls teasing out the tangles and pulling damp tendrils of hair over his ears stretching them into soft waves. She watched recognising a long time habit and not an insignificant amount of vanity in him. "Are you okay now?" He asked cutting through her thoughts.

"What! Sorry what..."

"You were trembling earlier. Are you alright now? I forget how scary Goblins must look to humans." He had wandered over to her bed and sat down on the edge. "I don't want you to be frightened Amy. I wouldn't let anything happen to you."

"I know that and I'm glad you're here." She hesitated before saying, "I wonder what my mother would make of me? Would she be disappointed to see how wimpy her daughter turned out? I bet she would have wanted me to follow that long line of Monkshood fighters instead of painting landscapes to sell to tourists"

"She would most likely have been quite proud of the way you inflate your prices when you don't like someone." He said trying to lighten her mood. It worked, she smiled at him and he noticed that she had a dimple in her right cheek. Their eyes locked and for the second time she wondered what it might be like to kiss him. He cleared his throat and getting up from the bed commented, a little disconcerted she thought, "You've only had a couple of hours sleep. You must be tired. Shall I turn off the light?"

She wondered if he had picked up on her thoughts about kissing him and felt her cheeks begin to burn; but hadn't he said that she would have to consciously send messages to him for him to pick up on them and she was fairly certain that she hadn't. She lay back down pulling the duvet up to her chin as he reached across to switch off the bedside lamp plunging the room back into darkness. She heard him move across the room and waited for the sound of the armchair to creak as he sat down. After a moment or two she said softly, "Goodnight Mal...Thank you for being here."
He didn't answer at once and she guessed he was smiling to himself. At last he responded, "You're welcome...Goodnight Amy."

After the nights shocking events Amy was relieved when the following week saw no further apparitions of Goblins or other strange creatures from hell. Malchediel was however as vigilant as ever never letting Amy out of his sight. The morning following the Goblins nocturnal visit Stephen called into the shop at lunchtime to check up on her. He was horrified when he learned of the happenings at the cottage but he never made the mistake of offering help again. An uneasy truce existed between him and Malchediel. He only spoke to the Angel when he had to and for his part Mal treated him with indifference. Amy was exasperated by his insensitive winding-up of Stephen one day when he was asked if he wanted anything fetching from the bakery. Amy had already requested her choice of sandwich, and Stephen had turned to Mal for his request. "I'll have a cheese salad baguette please." He said, "Multi-grain not white and not cheddar cheese…erm…I'll have Wensleydale…no, make that Red Leicester, no salad cream, I'll have mayonnaise instead, tomato but no onion and cucumber with the skin taken off first. Oh! And low fat spread please." He added for good measure. To add insult to injury he then gave Stephen one of his winning smiles. Amy glared at him but Stephen refusing to be goaded turned to the door enunciating clearly for Malchediel to hear, "Right…Cheese salad roll it is then." As the door closed behind him Amy burst out laughing. "Serves you right." She threw at him. "You are positively evil. Give the guy a break and try to be nice to him." Malchediel responded with an impudent grin.

During their evenings together Malchediel attempted to discover the extent of Amy's Nephilim powers. Apart from the thought transference abilities that she had awakened she could not detect any other super-human capabilities. She declared that there was nothing else she could do. "Perhaps thought transference is the limit of my special powers."

"No." Mal answered, "I won't accept that. There is more that you can do, we just haven't discovered what it is yet. You're a Monkshood with centuries of their genetic makeup within you. Plus there is a reason why you are being targeted. You're seen as a threat for some reason and it's not just because you can speak through your thoughts. You haven't been trained to hone your gifts as you were growing up but I know they will manifest themselves eventually."

Amy shrugged disconsolately still unconvinced.

September turned into October bringing with it wet south westerly gales. The mornings started dark and misty, setting the mood for the rest of the day and Amy saw little reason to open the shop in such weather. The tourists had dwindled to the odd hardy hiker but they had little inclination to purchase a painting to slide into their rucksacks. Malchediel was missing his former companions and he hated the cold damp weather. The only compensation was Amy's company. They spent time walking the cliff paths if the weather permitted. They rarely saw the sun but occasionally the relentless low mist cleared enough for them to don warm jackets and venture out. When the low cloud descended again they returned home where Amy would fill the kitchen with delicious smells from baking whilst Malchediel sat watching. He wondered how humans tolerated this inactive life-style. He missed the cut and thrust of the frequent battles he and his three companions were involved in. The last couple of weeks' inactivity was taxing his patience and unlike Amy he was craving some…any action. When it came, the timing and location surprised him.

The inclement weather of the past ten days suddenly one day gave way to a morning of mild autumn temperatures. The mist had lifted and a weak watery sun shone from the palest of skies. Amy and Malchediel had been housebound for two days due to heavy unremitting rain and they were both keen to get out for some exercise. Amy suggested driving down to the Lizard Point and then a walk along the coastal path which afforded brilliant views across Mounts Bay. They had been walking for about an hour and were in the middle of a discourse about eighteenth century smuggling in the area. Amy was in mid-sentence about the particularly gory hanging of three local men found guilty of trafficking in smuggled French brandy when

Malchediel suddenly stopped walking drawing in a sharp breath. She too stopped in her tracks following his gaze along the path. There, some thirty metres or so away stood a solitary figure. They had been unable to see the tall man dressed all in black because of a bend in the path and had come upon him suddenly. *Get behind me!* Amy heard in her mind and she detected the urgency with which Malchediel had spoken the thought to her. She didn't need telling twice and she dodged quickly behind him standing on tip toe to look over his shoulder at the stationary figure. Slowly they advanced towards the man who was standing looking out to sea giving every indication that he was unaware of their presence. Amy kept pace with Malchediel but stayed concealed behind him as he had instructed. When they were within five metres of him the man slowly turned to them, a smile spreading across his face as if he were greeting old friends.

"Asmodeus." Malchediel said coldly.

"Malchediel." Came the reply, "It's been a long time." Amy had her first long look at the stranger who was clearly known to Malchediel. He was every bit as striking looking as Mal but whereas he was all golden and sun-kissed, the stranger who he had called Asmodeus was dark and brooding. Handsome in a dangerous way and, she noted most definitely another Angel.

Chapter Five

Standing so closely behind Malchediel, Amy could feel the hostility radiating from him. Some instinct told her that the stranger was definitely another Angel and it was clear that Malchediel knew him and despite the welcoming smile she felt threatened by him. Perhaps it was that the smile lingered around his mouth never reaching his eyes.

"My quarrel is not with you Malchediel." He suddenly spoke. "Give me the girl and walk away."
Amy gasped at his words. They had been spoken quietly in a cultured voice but they were chilling never the less.

"I think not." was Mal's curt reply.

"She is nothing to you…" there was now an edge to his voice, a definite threat. "Hand her over and you can go home. You know it's what you want. You're above all this guardian servitude. Where is your pride?"

Amy knew that with that last question he was taunting Malchediel. She was impressed when Mal refused to rise to the bait. "Talking of guardians I believe you may know the whereabouts of two of them." He replied coolly.

The dark stranger tilted his head to one side feigning a moment of deep thought. "Ahh yes…I believe I came across a couple of knuckle-heads." He smiled again but it was full of derision this time. He snapped his fingers and instantly at his side appeared two bedraggled creatures barely recognisable as Angels. One of them was holding up the other who appeared to be incapable of standing unaided. They both seemed to have been beaten savagely; the weaker of the two had damaged wings that trailed limply to the floor, missing dozens of feathers. Dragging her eyes away from their injuries Amy could see that they were chained together with heavy manacles. She felt Malchediel's body tense as he beheld the sorry condition of the two guardian Angels. He drew in a ragged breath. "You will pay for this!" he growled.

"Oh, p-e-r-l-e-a-s-e…."drawled Asmodeus nonchalantly regarding his manicured nails. "You can take them if you like. I grow tired of spending my evenings plucking his feathers." He cast a disdainful glance at the most seriously injured of the guardians. Then he turned his full attention to Malchediel. He was no longer smiling. His beautiful face took on a hard edge and he spoke slowly and clearly. "I want the girl. I am willing to wait…but not too long. If you resist me I will take her anyway and you will pay the penalty for defying me." He made to turn away but Malchediel spoke quickly fearing that he would disappear. "Why is she so important to you?"

Asmodeus turned a darkened look at him. His eyes narrowed and he snarled, "She's the last of the Monkshoods. I've eradicated all the others. When she's dead I will be avenged."

"Avenged of what?"

"Her mother…" and his voice oozed all the hatred of hell, "killed my mate. I will have her daughter's life in retribution. Think on my offer Malchediel, failure to hand her over willingly will mean the death of both of you. You have a few days to consider your options." Before Malchediel could utter another word, Asmodeus vanished leaving the three Angels and Amy standing on the cliff path. It was another few seconds before Malchediel's shoulders relaxed, the tension leaving his body following the disappearance of the Fallen Angel. Amy stepped out from behind him reaching for his hand. He looked down at her taking in her white pallor. He gave her hand a quick squeeze before striding over to the two guardians. She watched as he eased the weaker of the two into a sitting position on the coarse grass. She caught her breath as he shattered the chain binding them together using a beam of light flowing from the index and second finger of his right hand. Then he knelt beside the sitting figure and spoke in a language that Amy had never heard before. He seemed to be asking questions as they both appeared to be answering in one syllable dialogue. After a few moments he rested his hand upon the sitting Angel's shoulder in a kindly manner murmuring a few more words before stepping back and watching as they slowly faded and disappeared. He turned and walked back to her. "Will they be alright?" she asked her voice cracking with emotion.

"They will be when they get home. Raphael will heal their injuries."

"They suffered all that because of me." She said simply.

"It comes with the job Amy. You were the reason not the cause. Angels heal quickly...they will recover."

"Why did he have to torture them?"

"Asmodeus always gave in to his cruel side. After Lucifer, he was one of the first to fall from grace."

"What are you going to do now?" she asked and he heard the tremor in her voice. He looked at her face and saw that her eyes were filled with tears. "I'm going to protect you." He said.

"But he said that he would kill us both."

"He can try."

"I'm scared. I don't doubt your abilities but he said that he has killed other members of my family...Oh God!" she said suddenly, "Do you think he was responsible for the death of both my parents?"

Malchediel shrugged. "It's possible. There were no witnesses to either of your parents' accidents. As to the verdict of your mother having been the victim of a hit and run driver, he is quite capable of making her murder appear that way." He saw a tear slowly gather on her lower eyelid and roll down her cheek. He reached forward and brushed it away with his thumb. "Come on let's go home. He won't do anything immediately. He's hoping to build on our anxiety for a while now. I know how he works." They turned back the way they had come retracing their steps, all thoughts of a leisurely walk forgotten.

"Do you know what he meant about my mother killing his mate? Does he mean his girlfriend...his partner?"

"Asmodeus is a lecherous character. He had several partners as you call them even before he fell. I can only imagine that his immorality worsened after he had been cast out."

"I don't understand. I thought Angels were all purity and goodness." She said in surprise.

He laughed glad that at least she wasn't still thinking about the death of her parents. "We are. There is nothing impure about forming relationships with members of our own kind. Our females can't reproduce which is fortunate. With us being immortal Heaven would be overrun with Angels; but we can and do enjoy sex."

Amy stared at him. "Wow...I hadn't realised." She looked away quickly not wanting him to see her embarrassment as she asked, "Is there someone special in your life at the moment?"

"At the moment..."he repeated with a smile, "No Amy, no one special."

"Right."

They walked on for a while in silence both wrapped up in their own thoughts. Malchediel's thoughts were focussed on what Asmodeus might do next. He didn't think he would waste time sending any more Demons or Goblins to torment them. He was pretty certain that he would handle the next attack himself. He had no illusions about the Fallen Angels' power. He had been a high ranking Angel in Heaven and no less so after following Lucifer to Hell. There was no way he was going to tell Amy how formidable an opponent he would prove to be. He knew whatever lay ahead, he was going to need all his skills to bring about Asmodeus' defeat...and there was no guarantee that he would win. By the time they reached Amy's car parked on the gravel parking area above the Lizard Point lifeboat station Malchediel was relieved to see that the colour was returning to her cheeks. She reached into her coat pocket for her keys, fumbled and dropped them, picked them up but had difficulty trying to insert it into the door. Malchediel watched and noted the tremor in her hands. He eased the key from her grip, happen I'll be glad of his celestial prowess. They fight differently to us mortals." She said with a hesitant smile.

"I worry about you Amy." He said giving her hand a gentle squeeze.

"Don't mind me." They heard Malchediel's voice from the doorway. They both turned to see him standing leaning casually against the door frame. He was smirking clearly enjoying Amy's discomfiture at being caught with her hand in Stephens. She pulled it away hastily as Malchediel continued, "Thanks for the tea." He rocked the mug to and fro indicating that it was empty. He walked across the kitchen and placed it in the sink. Turning back to them, he leaned against the edge of the cupboard. "Was there anything else?" He looked directly at Stephen who was clearly taken aback, not knowing what to say.

"I was just wondering if there was anything else that your father found other than Melissa's membership card?" he added with his most winning smile. Amy wasn't fooled. She knew when he was being sarcastic. This was his way of dismissing Stephen. Letting him know that it was time to leave. She could have hit him but instead she contented herself with glaring at him. It didn't help when he returned her look of annoyance with the most innocent of smiles.

"No, no. I just thought Amy would like to see her Mother's Nephilim I.D. card." Ignoring Malchediel, Stephen smiled at Amy. "If anything else turns up I'll let you know." He turned to leave fixing Malchediel with a less than friendly look. Amy followed him to the front door leaving Mal in the kitchen. Once outside on the driveway Stephen glanced her way, "He doesn't make it easy to like him does he?"

"I know," she answered with an embarrassed smile, "I'm sorry, I think he chews razor blades for breakfast."
Stephen smiled at her comment.

"And he's on our side too. I'd hate to see how he treats his enemies." He leaned close to drop a quick kiss on her cheek. She had never noticed it before but she was sure he was wearing aftershave. The realisation made her smile. She didn't want to give him any encouragement so as soon as he was in his car she walked back to the front door and without turning back entered the hallway. Malchediel was standing with his back to the fireplace, examining her mother's card. He looked up as she entered the room quickly taking in her look of disapproval. "What?" he asked feigning bewilderment.

"You know 'What?'" she answered. You can't resist goading him can you?"

He grinned, "I haven't had so much fun in centuries."

"Well...stop it I find it all very embarrassing. He's a good friend and you are very rude to him."

He didn't answer but kept up the grin until she, in spite of her annoyance with him couldn't stop her mouth from quirking upwards in response. "I'm serious." She said trying to keep her face straight. "Just for me, try to be civil to him will you?"

His face took on a look of chastisement, "Just for you, will try."

She found herself looking into his mischievous blue eyes and felt that familiar fluttering sensation in the pit of her stomach that had nothing to do with hunger and everything to do with latent attraction. She pulled her eyes away from him and in an attempt to cover the confusing sensations coursing through her, she walked quickly into the kitchen and began to fill the sink with water to wash up the mugs. Had she stayed she may have seen that Malchediel was also experiencing confusing emotions of his own. He too, had been aware of a brief electrical charge of attraction as their eyes had locked. He had watched her as she entered the kitchen and was now lost in thought absently tapping her mother's membership card against his chin. He was no stranger to emotions of the heart. He had lived for millennia and had experienced physical attraction many times. He believed he had even been in love more than once but always before, his liaisons had been with other Angels, ethereal beings like him, self-assured and confident, ever vigilant of their own well-being. Amy was different. She may have been a Nephilim, a half Angel but she had never been made aware of it and so outwardly she was like any other human, fragile. That vulnerability had awakened in Malchediel a strong sense of protection. It was an emotion he had never experienced before and it unsettled him. He was a warrior, initially railing against having to guard a human girl but now his sole aim was to safeguard her. On the cliff path earlier that day he had realised that he was no longer defending her because he had been assigned to the task...he was doing it because he wanted to. Her safety was important to him – he cared for her. He glanced up as she came back into the room. She was looking down at her hands, rubbing them together and he could smell the flowery fragrance of her hand cream. In the instant before she looked up at him he observed how her jeans hugged the contours of her hips. His eyes travelled up to her face. Her own eyes hidden by her auburn fringe, but then she casually pushed her hair behind her ears glancing his way and smiled at him. She held out her hand for her mother's membership card. "I wonder if you can still get through to that telephone number?" she asked. He was bought out of his reverie by her voice. "Try it." He suggested.

"I will." She said with a little giggle. "What do I say if someone answers?" she added, reaching for the phone beside the sofa. His eyes were drawn once again to the soft rounded shape of her hips before she straightened up with the phone in her hand.

"Tell them who you are and see what transpires."

It was with some disappointment that Amy listened to the unobtainable tone. She replaced the receiver before commenting, "I suppose after all this time I was expecting too much. Their number was bound to have changed. That card was issued to my Mum in her maiden name. That's well over twenty years ago." She was thoughtful for a minute or two before adding, "Even if I had spoken to someone they probably wouldn't have remembered a Melissa Monkshood."

She didn't sleep well that night. She lay in bed talking quietly to Malchediel in the darkened room. She asked him if he thought Asmodeus would honour his word and give them a few days before making a move against them.

"The only thing one can be sure of with Asmodeus is his unpredictability. I would think that he will delay any attack just to build on our anxiety but I recall that he never did what was expected so we need to be ready for anything."

His comment didn't instil any confidence in her. A silence descended on the room but after a little while she spoke again. "I'm really glad you're here Mal." She said her voice barely above a whisper. "I want you to know that whatever happens I'm aware that this isn't your fight and you could walk away from it right now." She took a deep breath adding, "It means a lot to me to know that you're here with me."

It was a moment or two before he answered. "I'm not the sort to walk away Amy. I was sent here to do a job." He hesitated choosing his next words carefully, "Since I got to know you it's become more than that...it's now personal."

She turned her head towards where he sat. She could detect nothing of his features, it was too dark but she could see the outline of his body sitting upright in the armchair. She mulled over what he had said. What did he mean, '*it's now personal.*' She was aware of her own feelings towards him. Could he possibly have feelings for her as well or was she reading more into his words than were intended. Could he just be bristling from Asmodeus insult regarding his lack of pride in becoming her Guardian? He was saying no more so she was left unsure. The night passed with no incidence and she awoke heavy eyed from lack of sleep and with a thumping headache.

The next week passed much the same. They stayed at home not venturing out. If an attack came Malchediel wanted it to be where he felt he had more control. Outdoors was too risky. He was handling the tension far better than Amy. After five consecutive nights tossing and turning she was irritable, pale and tired. She was almost wishing that something would happen to break the tension she was feeling.

Ten days after their cliff-top meeting with Asmodeus, he made good his promise and all Hell broke loose.

Chapter Six

As expected he made his move at night. It was a little before nine o'clock and Amy was putting away the clean laundry. She was standing on the landing at the open doorway into the airing cupboard stacking the clean towels onto the shelves when she thought she heard a noise coming from the bedroom. It didn't strike her as a suspicious sound; it was too soft to initiate any concern within her. It seemed as though it were a hissing or a flapping noise and her immediate thought was that a bird had entered through an open window and was frantically trying to escape. Leaving the remainder of the laundry in the basket she moved to the bedroom and slowly, so as not to panic the bird further, opened the door. There was a sudden flash of flame and she instantly felt the searing heat of fire. Instinctively she pulled the door to again, screaming Malchediel's name as she staggered backwards against the wall behind her. With Seraphic speed Malchediel was up the stairs and beside her. "Fire!" she yelled, "The bedroom is on fire!" She was waving her hand towards the door a look of panic on her face. Malchediel placed one hand flat against the door pulling it quickly away as he felt the heat through the wood. "It's him!" he hissed through clenched teeth.

"What? Who? You mean Asmodeus? How could he have set fire to my bedroom?"

"That's not a real fire." He exclaimed, "He's conjured it to scare and confuse." He uttered an expletive that was none too Angelic before opening the door just far enough to slip through closing it swiftly behind him. Amy shrieked as the heat rushed out onto the landing before throwing herself against the closed door. "Mal! Mal!" she cried beating upon the wooden panelled door. The door opened and Malchediel stood looking at her his eyes going up to her raised fists. "I didn't know you cared so much." He grinned. She looked past him into the room. There was no fire, no damage...not even a wisp of smoke. Everything looked as it should. "I told you. It wasn't a real fire." As he spoke they both turned to another sound coming from downstairs. The smile died on Malchediel's face as he pulled Amy behind him. "It's started." He said grimly. "Stay behind me." He said shortly as he came out of the bedroom onto the landing. He strode to the top of the stairs with her close at his heels. There was a cacophony of noise coming from below as though a gaggle of hooligans was smashing plates and throwing chairs and other items of furniture about. "Oh God! Oh God!" Amy kept repeating. "What the hell is he doing?" She came up abruptly behind Mal as he stopped at the head of the stairs looking down into the hallway below. His hand came behind him to steady her. She managed to peer around him to glimpse a couple of the ugly squat Goblins that had attacked Malchediel in the garden. They were crouched at the foot of the stairs chattering to each other in their strange guttural language. They looked up at him and the chattering stopped instantly only to be replaced by an even more bizarre snarling sound. "Oh don't be shy boys." Mal called to them mockingly. "Come on...let's see how brave you can be." Under his breath he added, "Or stupid."

The first started to mount the stairs, not an easy task given his short squat legs. "That's it, come on up." Mal coaxed an instant before dispatching it with a laser flame from his hand. The second Goblin watched as his companion exploded and disappeared in a cascade of gore. Before it had a chance to react Malchediel sent another flash to kill the second one too. Within seconds they were replaced by at least another dozen all clamouring to mount the stairs in an attempt to overpower the Angel and his human companion. "Oh you stupid, stupid creatures." Mal uttered as he eliminated one after another until the hallway was empty and quiet once more. Amy was holding onto the back of his shirt, the fabric gripped between her fingers. He looked over his shoulder at her taking in her fearful wide eyed gaze. "Are you alright?" he asked. She was unable to form words, she just nodded. He stood listening for a moment. When he was satisfied that there were no more Goblins lurking in the hallway he turned to her taking her hand in his. "Back into the bedroom Amy." He ordered. "We're too vulnerable out here."

She didn't need telling twice. She made for the bedroom door at a trot, Malchediel following. Once inside He slammed the door. "Over in the corner." He commanded. "And stay down. Don't get up unless I tell you to." She scuttled over to the corner of the room where he had indicated and crouched down backing well into the small space between the wall and the wardrobe. All was quiet and as her eyes became used to the darkened room she watched as he stood stock still listening with his head cocked to one side. There was not a sound other than her ragged breathing. Malchediel didn't seem unnerved in any way following the skirmish on the landing. His own breath was slow and measured. She jumped when Malchediel spoke suddenly. "What are you waiting for? Need time to conjure more assistance?" His voice was met with silence. He tried again. "Come on Asmodeus. It isn't like you to be so reticent. Do I detect a certain reluctance to face a Warrior?" Again, silence but then Malchediel's goading got a result. A disembodied voice filled the room. "You haven't made a wise choice Malchediel. You should have taken my offer to walk away. That offer is now rescinded. Foolish, very foolish."

Amy at once recognised the cultured voice. Her blood seemed to run cold through her veins. She watched Malchediel's back. He turned slightly towards the window and in a movement too fast for Amy to follow he raised his right hand in that direction and a warm blue light instantly lit that section of the room. Caught in the light was the hazy outline of Asmodeus standing looking straight back at Malchediel. "That's better." Malchediel murmured almost conversationally, "I do so hate talking to nothingness." Asmodeus gave a start to be suddenly made visible almost magically. Amy caught her breath at the power of Malchediel's arsenal of Angelic weaponry. She wondered what other tools this Angel could call upon. Asmodeus instantly regained his composure. "Whatever." He shrugged and with a snap of his fingers his hazy outline became solid. He leaned to one side looking around Malchediel at Amy's crouched figure and she flinched as their eyes met. "Ah, the little Monkshood." He drawled.

Malchediel stepped to the right cutting off the other Angels view of the crouching terrified girl. "Haven't you killed enough of her family? For Heaven's sake leave her alone. She's done nothing to you."

"For Heaven's sake?" Asmodeus mimicked the phrase. "For the sake of Heaven. Ah my old home. Closed to me now." He added, a definite touch of malice in his voice. "I don't think so. I have waited a long time Malchediel. I will have my revenge." He smiled, a cold upturning of the lips. "And you will have died for nothing." In the blink of an eye he raised his arm hurling three razor sharp spinning stars at Malchediel. Just as fast the Warrior Angel held up his own right hand twisting his fingers to the right. The murderous metal stars halted in mid-flight dropping harmlessly to the floor.

"Not bad." Drawled Asmodeus. "Try this..." and with a flick of the wrist he sent a sheet of flame aimed at Malchediel's chest. Again Malchediel parried the fiery threat holding both palms outstretched. The flame instantly disappeared leaving a wisp of blue smoke to travel upwards that too disappeared before it touched the ceiling. Asmodeus' shoulders slumped in mock resignation "Oh this could go on all night. I grow weary and there is a delightful little human female waiting for me elsewhere." He stood up straight and fixed Malchediel with a steely glare. "Let us finish this now." He said; a cold sense of finality to his voice.

"And I thought you were still mourning your murdered partner." Malchediel answered with equal iciness.

With a roar of anger Asmodeus drew back his arm as a

from the bed, his wings stretching to their full extent as first one then a second later two more Angels appeared to walk through the still closed door. She screamed in shock at the sudden appearance of the three figures. Her immediate thought was that they were Fallen Angels but then instinctively she considered that they didn't have the same presence that Asmodeus had displayed. With lightning speed Malchediel launched himself at the first Angel who equally quickly dodged to one side as he shouted something to his two companions in the language that Amy had come to recognise as Angelic possibly Aramaic. In response, the two caught hold of Malchediel by his upper arms holding him in a grip he could not escape. He was shouting at them in a rage that she had never witnessed before even in the heat of battle with the Goblins of Hell. The Angel who appeared to be in charge turned from Malchediel who was struggling against his captors to look at Amy and she cowered back against the headboard of the bed. Realising that she was naked from the waist up, she quickly pulled the duvet up against herself. Malchediel had stopped his futile struggling but was still shouting at them in anger. The Angel had to raise his voice to be heard over the noise. He spoke to Amy in English. "My name is Nemamiah. Perhaps Mal has spoken of me."

Amy nodded dumbly. Malchediel had ceased his tirade as Nemamiah spoke, then with a coldness that shocked Amy he said, "You're too late Nem. I couldn't go back now even if I wanted to." Amy watched as Nemamiah slowly turned back to look at Malchediel. In a voice filled with sadness Nemamiah spoke again. "Oh No...please no Mal don't say that."

Mal's voice at variance with his friends positively dripped with contempt, "It's true. Use your eyes, what do you see?"

Nemamiah turned back to Amy taking in the tumbled duvet, her naked shoulders above the bedclothes and her flushed cheeks. He let out a sigh. "Is it true?" he asked quietly. "Have you consummated your union?"

ability to conjure flames and beams of light from them. That was the last objective thought to enter her head as she gave herself up to his increasingly urgent caresses. With his hands still encircling her hips and his lips on hers he slowly backed her up until the backs of her knees came up against the bed. The sudden contact made her legs buckle but he held her firmly allowing her to sink down easily onto the mattress. She moved backward easing her legs up as he pulled his sweater up over his head, then as she watched he unzipped his jeans kicking them free before kneeling next to her on the bed. He leaned forward supporting himself on outstretched hands either side of her and kissed her once more before drawing back to take the hem of her pyjama top lifting it upwards. She raised her arms allowing him to pull it up over her head. Suddenly exposed to his gaze she felt embarrassed and attempted to cross her hands across her chest in a belated act of modesty. He smiled at her and she felt her cheeks grow hot. Gently he took her arms and lowered them keeping his eyes on her face. He spoke to her in the same language that he had used before and she thought that she had never heard anything so melodious before. It was like music to her ears. He bent to kiss her throat, a kiss so feather light she barely felt it. His lips wandered down across her shoulder leaving her breathless. Her hands were against his chest and he felt her body yielding in response to him. She turned her head resting her own lips against his hair delighting in the soft silky feels of the tousled curls brushing her face. Her eyes were closed as she whispered, "I love you." Then again with a sigh, "I love you." Suddenly with a ferocity that made her eyes fly open he pulled himself away from her turning with incredible speed completely around to stare across the bottom of the bed. He was on hands and knees looking away from Amy with an intensity that made her cry out in surprise. He appeared to be looking towards the door leading out onto the landing. Inexplicably, for there was nothing to see, he let out a howl of rage. Amy sat transfixed staring at his back where his wings were beginning to unfurl. In one swift movement he had leaped before him. Amy had opened his mind to other possibilities...but wasn't that the human way? He wasn't human. He didn't have free will; he didn't have the luxury to choose the path his life should take. He was an Angel after all and it was his duty to obey but he was beginning to realise that to have a choice over one's life was an attractive notion. He needed to stop this chain of thought. Standing up he walked away from Amy to view what she had sketched so far. She stayed where she was sitting on the jetty looking out along the river thinking not so much about his mixed feelings about the time when he would be called back home but how she would react when that time came.

choice. Angels do not have free will. We do as we are told. I can't dictate where I live." He looked across at her and smiled sadly.

"But what would happen," she repeated, "if you just didn't return?"

"I would be recalled against my will to answer a charge of insubordination. There is no way I could fight it. I would instantly appear before a court of elders."

"You mean you would be hauled bodily back from here and you would have no say in the matter."

"Exactly." He smiled ruefully.

"And if you told them that you didn't want to stay there, would they imprison you?"

He looked away from her to gaze back down the river.

"No...that's not how it works. Once an Angel declares that he no longer wants to be a part of the Celestial family he or she is cast adrift, to wander for all eternity. There would be no re-admittance. It would be as if they had never existed. You then join the ranks of the Fallen."

"But that is so cruel Mal. The Fallen are evil. You could never be like one of them. How could they treat you like the worst sort of criminal?"

"You miss the point Amy. It would be my choice. My choice to turn my back on my family. As long as I abide by the rules I would have a home and a family. I would only be abandoned if I told them that I wanted to leave." Before she had a chance to comment there was a sudden screeching noise accompanied by a flurry of movement and flapping of wings as a pheasant took flight from the tree line heading across the river in front of them. It was enough of a distraction to break the mood of sombre elucidation of his position in his celestial family. It also gave him pause to wonder if he had revealed too much regarding his confusion over when or even if he should return home. He had never before questioned his own feelings about being a Warrior Angel. He just was and he had always accepted whatever mission was put to check when there is a next full moon. Moonlight reflecting on the water can be magical." She was looking off into space clearly visualising the scene. He watched her in silence. After a moment she came back down to earth and smiled at him. "Yes...The Helford River it is then."

When Malchediel saw Amy's chosen location he was captivated by the scenery. As she set up her equipment on a small wooden jetty he walked along the river bank surveying the sights and sounds of the river. There were three or four fishing boats moored along the far bank. The only life he could see were water fowl...a few ducks and a solitary swan gliding effortlessly past the bobbing craft. He walked to the bend in the river and then turned around to wander back to the jetty. By the time he reached Amy she had set up her easel and had started to draw the scene before her. Without a word he sat down on the wooden boards a foot or so away from her and gazed back up the river focussing on the swan as it slowly passed from view around the bend. "It's beautiful here. Is it always this quiet?" he asked.

Without pausing in her sketching she answered, "That's why I like to come here. I think it has to be my favourite place in the whole world." When he didn't answer, she looked towards him the pencil stilled in her hand. He was watching her with an intensity that made her catch her breath. "What is it?" she asked her voice barely above a whisper.

He dragged his eyes from her face and looked back along the river. He sighed, "The longer I stay here Amy the more difficult it's going to be to leave." There he had said it. He had put into words what he had been thinking since he had returned from his Celestial home. It was shocking to hear his own words but it was how he felt.

She laid her pencil down and stepped towards him sitting down beside him. "What would happen if you told them that you weren't going back?" she asked.

He gave a mirthless laugh. "Ohh Amy as if I had a

He nodded. "If you are ever in danger...if you ever need me I will know it." He covered her hand with his own, the feather held upright against her chest. "I will come." He said simply. She looked away from him across the room towards the French doors and the garden beyond so overcome with emotion that she couldn't look him in the eye. He continued to look at her profile fighting the impulse to take her in his arms and kiss her. Before he had a chance to act upon such a disastrous inclination she turned away from him. He watched as she walked to the book case. Opening the drawer she placed the feather carefully on top of the folded table napkins and closed the drawer. She stood for a few seconds with her back to him composing herself. His gesture of giving her the feather had moved her more than he could ever know. She took a deep breath, "A glass of wine?" she suggested and without waiting for an answer she made her way to the kitchen leaving him to marshal his own confused thoughts.

The following day he recommended taking a break from practising her telepathic skills and she was more than happy to agree to his suggestion to take her painting equipment and spend some time relaxing with her favourite hobby. "Won't you be bored?" she asked. "You'll just be watching me. Not very exciting for you."

"We Angels enjoy a little R and R at times too. We can talk and I can criticize if I don't like what you're painting." He added with a smirk.

She dismissed his suggestion of returning to Gunwalloe and said that for some time she had been thinking of producing a pair of canvases depicting the same scene, one during the daytime and one at night. She explained that she had seen another Cornish artist's work using this technique and had been impressed.

"So, do you have a location in mind?" he asked.

"Yes." She answered, "There's a little spot on the Helford River that is equally stunning by day and by night. I need with me." She said soberly.

"That's not possible though Amy. This isn't my world. I have already stayed longer than I should have." He wondered if she had any inclination that this was going to be just as difficult for him. He had never formed an attachment for a mortal before and the depth of his feelings shocked him.

"Do you think our paths will ever cross again? You know, once you have returned home. Is that how you see it? Home I mean." There was a slight tremor in her voice and it hurt him to hear it. He wanted to reach for her hand but that would be the worst thing he could do right now. He knew she was holding back on the tears. "Yes, I suppose you could call it my home although I'm often away from it and...yes, I truly hope that our paths will cross again Amy." He drew in a breath before going on. "I'm going to do something I've never done before. Raguel would have seven kinds of fit if he knew about it." He reached for the hem of his sweater and in one movement pulled it over his head, then standing up he flexed his shoulders and unfurled his magnificent wings. Amy watched in amazement. Although she had seen him do it before she looked on in awe as the creamy appendages opened fully. When Malchediel reached behind himself to pluck one of the larger feathers she winced. He glanced at her pained expression and grinned. After a moment she returned a smile of her own, "Oh...that had to have hurt." She said. His grin broadened as he recognised the words that he had uttered the very first time they had met. He smoothed the feather between his forefinger and thumb before holding it out to her. The smile slowly faded from his face. "Keep this safe Amy." He said and as she took it from him he added, "If ever you should need me just break the shaft. Snap it completely, I'll be able to sense it and I'll come as quickly as I can."

Taking the feather she held it by its calamus aware of the sticky secretion where it had been plucked from his wing. "You can do that?" she asked, astonishment in her voice, "You will be able to sense it if I were to snap the shaft?"

Within a few days Malchediel's shoulder had healed leaving little more than a puckered scar to add to the many other silvery thread-like marks across his body. Amy was dismayed to learn that rapid healing was one attribute that was peculiar to Angels and not shared by Nephilim. "That's not fair." She pouted, "Why wasn't that gene passed down to us?"

Malchediel grinned at her. "All Nephilim are hybrids, a mixture of human and Angelic blood. You can't have it all."

"I would say we got a raw deal." She grumbled. "The two best traits, rapid healing and the ability to fly...you lot kept for yourselves."

"You humans have enough problems driving automobiles. What you would be like if you took to the air goodness knows." He laughed. That comment earned him a black look.

To hone her telepathic skills Malchediel schooled himself to hold certain thoughts in his mind allowing Amy to try to detect what he was thinking. This was fine for a while but after a full day of this basic training she became bored with the mundane thoughts that she was picking up from him. "This is getting boring. What's so interesting about your favourite poem or which country you hope you never have to visit again? This is all too contrived Mal." Her eyes took on a mischievous glint, "Now how about what **you** fear the most...that would be more interesting." And before he had a chance to mask his thoughts she tapped into his mind. "Whoa-ho-ho." She cried gleefully, "You fear losing your looks. How vain is that?" she laughed.

"Yes...well..." he blustered more than a little embarrassed. "I wasn't prepared for that. You play dirty, little Nephilim." They had been sitting across from one another in the living room and they looked at each other smiling at the shared joke. Seconds passed, the smiles faded and Amy spoke, "I shall miss you Mal...when you have to leave. I wish you could stay was you who killed Asmodeus, not Malchediel."

"Stephen!" Alex said sharply clearly embarrassed by his son's bold outburst. Amy flashed a quick look towards Malchediel taking in his hot flush of humiliation.

"Mal was impaled by Asmodeus's spear and that was my fault. I distracted him by screaming otherwise he would have been the one to have killed him."

Stephen made no further comment. He didn't have to. All three of them were left in no doubt that he felt Malchediel had let Amy down leaving her to protect herself. The Angel and the teenager gave each other a hard look. It was Malchediel who looked away first. Alex asked if they could see where the confrontation with Asmodeus took place. Amy led them upstairs to her bedroom. Malchediel stayed downstairs. As Amy followed Alex and Stephen into the hallway she turned briefly back to him and smiled re-assuringly at him. She felt that Stephen's comments were unfair and were only uttered out of chagrin. In the bedroom it was clear that both Alex and Stephen were shocked upon seeing the javelin still jammed firmly in the doorframe. Amy had a fleeting sense of requital on Mal's behalf when Stephen tried but failed to pull the spear free. It took both him and his father to wrench it out with a splintering of wood. As he held it weighing it carefully afterwards, Amy was gratified to see that he was now aware what Malchediel had gone through for her sake. On their return to the living room he surprised Amy by openly apologising to Malchediel. "I hope you will forgive my earlier comments. I was out of order. Seeing that spear...well...sorry. It must have been bloody agony."

Malchediel, after a moment's hesitation smiled back,

"Yes it was." Amy was relieved that by the time Alex and Stephen left, the atmosphere between Malchediel and the younger Goodrich was, if not exactly friendly certainly more amiable than it had been earlier

"What I actually said was that as long as Asmodeus had been working alone it was probably over now. I can't see how your life will ever be 'normal' from now on. You can't just shut down your new found abilities. They're there whether you like it or not Amy."

"But I don't want to be able to see into peoples' minds. It's abnormal. I didn't ask for this. I just want to be a normal human being. The thought of being able to kill someone scares me witless." He was still holding her by her upper arms and he looked into her agitated face with a semblance of compassion. "Ohh Amy," he said with feeling. "One thing you are not is a normal human being. You are what you are…a Nephilim. You are part Angelic and that cannot be changed. You may be able to pretend to live as a human but you will always have the power to protect yourself and your loved ones. You just need to be careful how far you use that power."

After a moment's hesitation she nodded her head acknowledging his words but not liking them.

Later that day Amy telephoned Alex Goodrich and explained that there had been a confrontation with Asmodeus at her cottage overnight and both she and Malchediel needed to speak to him. Would he be kind enough to call and see her as soon as possible? Once he had satisfied himself that she was alright he confirmed that he would be there within the hour. He arrived with Stephen who he had picked up from the shop on the way. She opened the door and led them into the living room giving Malchediel a look that encompassed the message; *Stephen is here as well…Be nice!!*

Both father and son listened in silence as Amy relayed the previous evening's happenings. There was a moment's silence as she finished with, "Malchediel explained later that when Angels die their bodies vaporise which was why there was the blinding flash of light before he disappeared."

"Let me get this right." Stephen said with a frown, "It

splintered wood She lifted her hand intending to take hold of it to see if she could pull it free, but froze when she saw the dried blood on the shaft. Malchediel's blood. She gave an involuntary gasp as she remembered the grotesque sight of him impaled by the vicious spear.

"Good! You're awake."

She spun around at the sound of his voice. He was standing in the doorway holding two mugs of steaming tea. He looked wonderful to her, not at all as he should following what had occurred a few hours earlier. He just had time to put the mugs down on the dresser by the door before she threw herself into his arms holding onto him as though her life depended on it. He was still wearing just the pair of jeans that he had on the night before and he could feel her hot tears on his chest. "Hey...hey what's this all about?" He stroked her hair as she clung to him knowing that at last the enormity of what had gone on in this room the night before had finally overwhelmed her. He waited and after a couple of hiccups she spoke. "I don't know why I'm hugging you. Since you came into my life my world has turned upside down."

He laughed and squeezed her before holding her at arms' length. Her eyes immediately fell on the dressing on his shoulder-not the one that she had applied a few hours ago. She looked up at him questioningly. "Hmm," he said wondering what she would say upon learning that he had returned home during the night. "Whilst you were asleep I was summoned home."

She caught her breath, "And you were allowed to come back here again?" she said in astonishment.

Taking a deep breath he answered. "I'm to give you instruction. They allowed me to return whilst you learn how to deal with your new telepathic powers."

She drew back in surprise. "I was hoping that I wouldn't need to use these 'new powers' as you call them. I thought you said that now Asmodeus is no longer around, my life could return to normal."

Raguel spoke for the first time, "Considering your reluctance to accept this task initially you seem to have adapted extremely well."

Malchediel tensed at his words. *Tread carefully.* He warned himself. "It is true I was reluctant to work with this girl at first but you insisted Raguel and you have to admit that I don't shirk my responsibilities." His expression was completely open and Raguel had no option but to desist. The older Senate member spoke again. "Are you willing to return and give instruction to this young Nephilim girl Malchediel?"

Malchediel shrugged as nonchalantly as he could, "If that is your wish I will do what I can."

He could hardly believe how things had worked out. Within an hour he was ready to leave once more with the blessing of the elders. He was so pleased with the outcome that any feeling of guilt at his duplicity was firmly pushed to the back of his mind. He knew that he would eventually have to face up to the dishonest way he had handled the matter but not yet. He was on his way back to Amy and that was all he could think about at the moment.

She was still asleep as he re-entered the room. Slowly he retracted his wings sending a silent 'thank you' to Raphael for the pain numbing balm that he had applied to the javelin wound. He gently eased himself onto the bed smoothing the throw over him. He smiled into the darkness as Amy gave a little snort turning onto her side so that her face came up against his neck. He froze barely breathing as she settled against him without waking then he too slipped into an Angelic slumber.

When Amy awoke the following morning the bed next to her was empty. Pushing herself up on one elbow she scanned the room. Her eyes locked on the steel javelin embedded in the doorframe. Images of what had happened the previous evening flooded her mind and in an instant she was off the bed and making for the weapon protruding some two feet from the transported back much the same as the two Guardian Angels had been. If that happened there would be no warning… No Goodbyes to Amy. She would just wake up to find him gone. He couldn't do that to her. He needed time. He would have to return of his own free will. Perhaps he could bargain for more time with her. If he went back now he could allay any suspicion as to his motives. He slipped from the bed. She murmured but slept on. He found it painful to unfurl his wings; perhaps the javelin had damaged some of his feathers. He would ask Raphael to inspect them when he got home. Without a sound he passed through the wall and headed heavenward.

On his return he went straight to Raphael's surgery. The Angelic healer commented on the efficiency of Amy's dressing but was disappointed that she had been unable to ease the pain of the javelin wound. Within minutes he had applied a balm that instantly gave complete relief. "You were lucky Malchediel. There is no damage to your wings. The discomfort you felt when you extended them was just dried blood clogging them together." It was as he was bathing the clotted blood away that Raguel and two members of the Senate arrived to question him about the night's events.

They listened in silence as Malchediel gave them the details of Asmodeus's attack and Amy's part in his killing. "She had no idea how she was able to do it." He finished. "I have never seen anything like it before. Up until that point she was in denial that she possessed any Nephilim power at all."

The two investigating Angels spoke together in hushed tones before turning back to Malchediel. "What would be your recommendations regarding the girl. Would it be prudent to let her come to terms with this new found power under her own steam?" asked the older of the two.   "Given the power of her abilities I believe that would be unwise." Malchediel glanced at Raguel as he spoke noting the definite lift of his brow. He went on, "I think she needs instruction on how to come to terms with and how she should use these new abilities."

They wedged in the narrow tube of rising water making it impossible for him to float upwards allowing him those few extra moments of air. Amy glanced behind her taking in Malchediels reaction to what was happening. There was a look of astonishment mingled with the pain from his injury on his face. Her eyes dropped to his body quickly taking in the sickening sight of the javelin pinning him to the wall behind him. She tore her eyes away from his blood drenched shirt focussing back on the Fallen Angel, the water now at his chin. "Stop this now. Please. Tell me what you want. I can grant you anything. Just stop this." As he spoke the water swished around his mouth. With an effort he craned his neck as high as it would go. "Tell me what you want." He gurgled.

Coolly Amy answered, "I want you to die."

She watched as the water continued to rise, now level with his nose... his eyes. She could see his mouth still working but of course there was no sound. As the water reached the top of his head his mouth ceased working. A few bubbles escaped upwards... then nothing. Within a few seconds there was a blinding flash. Amy closed her eyes against the intensity of it. The room fell deathly silent. When she opened her eyes again the column of water had gone, as though it had never existed. There was no sign of Asmodeus. There was no trace of water, not even a patch of damp on the carpet. Amy stood still completely drained. The power that had been surging through her as she had willed the column of water around Asmodeus was completely depleted. She turned around to face Malchediel who stared back at her in wonder. "How did you do that?" His voice was dry and cracked. His hands were still gripping the javelin as he shook his head in disbelief. She staggered towards him, her limbs felt heavy and sluggish. "Oh my Darling. My darling." She gasped taking in his terrible injury. His shoulders were hunched, the spear protruding from his chest by more than six inches. "I'm alright, I'm alright. It's not serious." He tried to sound confident but he knew that to get free was going to cause even more excruciating pain. Amy stood in front of against the flow. What was this? He was standing facing her in her own bedroom laughing almost hysterically but all she could see was his terror as he was drowning. Then she recognised the vision for what it was. She was seeing the one thing that Asmodeus feared….Drowning. All at once she knew what her Nephilim power was. She had 'the sight'. She also knew that she had the power to act upon it. Striding from the corner of the room where she had been cowering in fear she approached him.

"Amy…NO…" Malchediel called to her. The javelin that he was still holding had lost its heat and was no longer glowing white hot. Asmodeus had forgotten all about it and was now solely focussed on Amy. "Amy…Yes." He mimicked Malchediel. "Come and meet your fate Nephilim."

"Ohh you are so going to wish you hadn't targeted the Monkshoods." She threw at him.

He laughed again unaware of the pool of water at his feet. It started to rise up around his shoes but instead of spreading outwards across the floor it seemed to be collecting in an invisible tube around his body. He was still laughing beckoning her towards him when he became aware of the water sloshing around his ankles and rising all the time. He lifted one leg looking down in bemusement as the water rose to his shins. The laughter died on his lips as he began to see what was happening. Amy kept her eyes on his face willing the water to rise up and up. He tried to step away from the water but came up against the invisible barrier. It was as though he was inside a glass tube just large enough to accommodate his body and all the while the water was rising. Now it was at his knees. His eyes were no longer full of gleeful malice. Now he felt fear and it showed in his eyes. "STOP IT! STOP IT!" He cried.

Amy's eyes glittered with hatred. "You're going to drown you bastard. This is for my mother, my father and all the other innocents you have killed."

As the water reached his chest he tried to unfurl his wings hoping to fly free of his watery prison. It was a mistake.

javelin formed in his hand. He hurled it at Malchediel. Amy screamed causing him to turn back towards her. Realising his error he swung back. Too late. He was unable to avoid the weapon hurtling towards him. He managed to straighten as it struck him in his left shoulder slamming him backwards against the wall. With a howl of pain he felt the weapon cut through flesh and muscle exiting through his back and impaling him against the door frame behind him. He was dimly aware of Asmodeus's cry of triumph mingled with Amy's long drawn out scream. Gritting his teeth against the pain he tried to pull his body forward in an attempt to free himself from the door behind him. He was held fast. He guessed that the javelin had a barbed head and there was no way he could pull himself free. He gripped the shaft of the javelin with both hands as a feeling of nausea swept over him. Asmodeus wasn't finished with him yet.

With an animal-like snarl he extended his arm pointing his index finger at the javelin. It immediately began to glow turning from cold metal to a white hot glowing rod of pure pain. Asmodeus's gleeful laughter was quickly drowned out by Malchediel's agonised scream.

"STOP IT! For God's sake stop it." Amy had risen from her knees in the corner and now stood with tears streaming down her face. "Ohh Malchediel…" she cried taking in his ashen face. He was still holding the javelin shaft and she could see smoke curling up from between his fingers. She could smell scorched flesh. Turning to face Asmodeus, a look of naked hate on her face she hissed "You bastard! He threw his head back and laughed and in that moment she looked into his eyes. Fear for herself had vanished. She stared at him and saw not his gleeful expression. What she saw was something quite different. She saw into his very soul. She shook her head trying to clear the image that came to her but it persisted. She saw him up to his neck in water. He was floundering in deep, deep water, his eyes huge and terrified. He held his head back trying to keep his face above the swirling water, his arms flailing

Amy was so taken aback by the question. She couldn't answer. Malchediel was not so reticent, "I told you..." he shouted, "They wouldn't want me back now anyway. I've broken all your rules." He started to laugh, an unnatural sound tinged with hysteria. "You came too late. We..."

Suddenly Nemamiah bellowed cutting off Malchediel's angry tirade, "SHUT UP MAL! BY ALL THE SAINTS JUST SHUT UP!"

Malchediel, breathing heavily, ceased his ranting. Nemamiah turned back to Amy. When he spoke his tone was quiet and gentle. "Amy this is the most important question you will ever be asked. Malchediel's very life depends upon your answer. If the two of you have made love then Mal has indeed broken our laws and will be banished from returning with us. For the rest of eternity he will be a Fallen Angel. Think about that. Is that what you want for him? Think about it and answer truthfully."

The room had fallen deathly quiet, the four Angels waiting for Amy's response. She looked past Nemamiah to Malchediel. He stood tense held between his two former companions. Slowly he shook his head at her willing her to lie...to give him the reason to stay with her. Her lips moved mouthing three words, 'I love you.' Then turning to Nemamiah she said quietly, "No, nothing happened...he has broken no rules."

Malchediel let out a long low moan of defeat.

Without hesitation and before Malchediel could protest Nemamiah hissed to the two Angels holding him. "Get him out of here!"

Within an instant Malchediel was being hauled struggling back towards the doorway. Before they disappeared he shouted, "I love you Amy. I'll always love you..." then they were gone. The suddenness of their exit shocked Amy and she was up immediately on hands and knees screaming Malchediel's name. There was no answer ...he had gone. With tears streaming down her face she turned to Nemamiah who was still standing immobile by the bed. "What will happen to him?" She sobbed. "Please don't hurt him…I told you the truth. He only kissed me…"

"Nothing will happen to him Amy. We aren't his enemies. We will cover for him. Here…" He said holding out her pyjama top. "Put this on." He turned away from her as she took the garment and scrambled into it. He faced her again. "May I?" he asked indicating that he wanted to sit on the bed next to her. She drew a ragged breath attempting to stop the sobs racking her body. He waited giving her time to compose herself. As she wiped the tears away with the back of her hand she nodded moving away so that he had room to sit. "We had to come Amy, questions were being asked. He had been summoned and he didn't reply. Better for him that it was us, his friends than others who wouldn't have been so lenient. I have known him for a very long time. I knew there was something going on. I am so very sorry for you but I think you know that you have done the right thing."

Amy said nothing; her misery was plainly etched on her face. Nemamiah took a deep slow breath before going on. "Amy…I need to ask you to do one more thing for me." He paused weighing his next words. "I know that Malchediel will try to return to you as soon as he can. We can't keep him locked up for ever…I need you to write a letter to him telling him that it's all over between the two of you. I need you to tell him not to contact you ever again…Will you do that…for his sake."

She looked at his face in disbelief as a tear slipped over her lower eyelid to roll slowly down her cheek. "I can't do that…" she said brokenly. "I can't forsake him. How could I possibly write a letter pretending that I don't love him?"

Nemamiah sat looking at her wondering what to say next. He reached for her hand and gently took it between his own two. Her eyes widened as she felt a ripple of electricity pass through her fingers. It was suddenly gone leaving her wondering if she had imagined it. "Please Amy; I need you to help me."

Slowly a sense of resolve formed in her mind. He was right. She knew Mal would take the first opportunity to return to her and all this would have been for nothing.

"I can't do what you want. I can't write to him but there is another way to achieve what you want." She swung her legs out of bed and without waiting to see if he was following her she went to the door and left the room.

Downstairs she went straight to the bookcase. Opening the drawer she picked up the creamy feather. She closed her eyes as she held it up feeling the tip lightly brush her chin. She was lost in thought remembering the day he had plucked it from his wing. She became aware of Nemamiah standing at her shoulder. She opened her eyes and turned to him. "Mal gave this to me and said…"

"I know." He interrupted. "I know why he would have given it to you."

She held it out to him. "You can tell him that I won't have need of it anymore. He'll understand" She said sadly. "It should be as effective as any 'Dear John' letter and at least I won't have to write any lies to him."

He took the feather from her. "Thank you Amy." He was about to turn away, hesitated and then sought her eyes. "I love him too Amy. I'm doing this for him. This was never meant to be…"

"I didn't choose for this to happen you know." She said sadly. "I'm quite aware of our differences. At least he won't have to see me growing old whilst he stays forever young. It would be unbearable…to see his love fade with my looks." She made an attempt to smile but he saw her lips tremble. She closed her eyes. "Please just go." She murmured her voice heavy with despair. She felt a movement of air and when she opened her eyes again she was alone in the room.

When Nemamiah reached his Celestial home he headed straight for Malchediel's room. As he turned into the corridor leading to the quarters containing the Warrior Angel's rooms he was met by Paschar and Qaphsiel. They were leaning against opposite walls facing one another. Nemamiah came up short upon seeing his two companions who appeared to be waiting for him. "Well?" he enquired. Paschar, hands in his pockets, looked down at his toes, not answering. Nemamiah turned a questioning gaze to Qaphsiel, who shrugged. "He's furious." He said simply. "I've never seen him like that before." He looked down the corridor to Malchediel's room. "It's quiet now but you should have heard him earlier. He turned his gaze back to Nemamiah. "The door is secure although he tried his hardest to get through. Are you going to try to speak to him Nem?"

Nemamiah sighed. "I suppose I have to."

Paschar looked up. "How is the Nephilim?"

"She'll be okay. It's him that I'm concerned about now. Hellfire I hope he can forgive what we did today."

Paschar and Qaphsiel exchanged knowing looks. Nemamiah rarely used expletives. It was evident that he was concerned about Malchediel's reaction when they next faced one another. Taking a deep breath he strode to Mal's door.

He turned the handle and entered the room. Malchediel who had been sitting on the floor, his back to the wall, jerked his head up from where it had been resting supported by his arms which were wrapped around his knees. He hadn't attempted to dress. He was still in the boxer shorts that he had been wearing in Amy's bedroom. When he saw Nemamiah standing before him he let out a howl of rage and jumping up slammed his friend against the wall, his arm across the other's throat. Nemamiah made no attempt to defend himself, his arms hanging motionless at his sides. The door beside him shuddered in its frame with the force of the attack. They were face to face, inches apart. Nemamiah took in Malchediel's angry expression. His blonde hair matted against his forehead, his face streaked with sweat. "Fight back, damn you!" he yelled. "I could kill you for what you've done!" Nemamiah remained calm looking his companion in the eyes. Quietly he asked, "Would that make you feel any better?"

Malchediel remained holding Nemamiah pinned against the wall for some seconds longer but then his grip relaxed and his arms too dropped to his sides. He stepped back allowing Nemamiah to survey the room beyond as he tentatively rubbed his bruised neck with his fingertips. "I see you've been remodelling the room." He said attempting a little humour. There was not one piece of furniture intact. Splintered wood and torn fabric littered the floor a testament to Malchediel's frenzied assault on his quarters after he had been locked in. Malchediel turned back glowering at his friend. "You can't keep me here forever Nem. I'll just go back to her as soon as I'm free." Nemamiah looked sadly at him. Reaching into his shirt he pulled out the feather and held it out. "She sent this back." He said.

Malchediel's eyes went to the feather. His jaw hardened as he looked up at his friend's face. "How did you get that?" he asked an edge to his voice.

"Mal..." he answered softly, "She gave it to me willingly. She said you would understand. She said she wouldn't need it anymore."

The two Angels eyed one another across the room, one consumed with compassion the other equally full of anguish and resentment. Eventually Malchediel spoke. "Get out! Get out Nem before I forget that you were once my friend." His voice resonated with icy intent. Nemamiah reached for the door knob and left the room without another word. As the door closed behind him there was a deafening crash as something heavy hit it from the other side.

No one approached Malchediel for the next two days. He was left alone. His three companions took it in turns to wait within earshot of his door but nothing was heard from within. On the third day Raguel asked Nemamiah for news of him.

When he was told that Malchediel had returned a few days earlier Raguel requested that Mal be told to report to the Overseer to make his report. Nemamiah covered Mal's absence by informing Raguel that he had been receiving treatment from Raphael for a damaged wing. Raguel looked up from the manuscripts on his desk giving Nemamiah a non-committal look before lowering his eyes back to his work. Nemamiah guessed that his excuse sounded flimsy but Raguel made no comment other than re-issuing his request for Malchediel to present himself before him.

There was nothing for it; Nemamiah had to pass the message on.

He hesitated before Malchediel's door before calling out, "Mal...it's me, can I come in?"

"I haven't locked it," came the reply.

Nemamiah swallowed hard before entering the room. Malchediel was standing at the window looking out over the gardens. He was fully clothed. He turned to face his companion and Nemamiah was shocked at his appearance. He looked older somehow, his face lined with dark shadows under his eyes. Nemamiah could only guess at the misery the other Angel was feeling. "I am truly sorry Mal." He said in a low voice. "But I still think we did the right thing."

Malchediel said nothing. Nemamiah went on, "Raguel has been asking after you."

"And you told him what? That I almost disgraced my celestial station? That I fell in love with a Nephilim and had to be dragged back here kicking and screaming." His voice was flat, the anger he had displayed three days ago was spent. There was a weary tone to his words as though he now accepted the inevitable.

Nemamiah was deeply moved and walked up to his friend who had once more turned to gaze out of the window. He placed a hand on the other's shoulder. "Mal...if I could take away your hurt I would. We have been friends for millennia and

I cannot bear to see you like this."

"I love her Nem. I have never felt this way before..." A solitary sob racked his body. Nemamiah waited and Malchediel composed himself before going on. "I know it's over now. She ended it by returning the feather." He straightened and turned to face his friend, "How was she when you left her?"

"I won't lie to you Mal. She was crying but she recognised your differences. She is a mortal. She knows that she will grow old and eventually die as all mortals do. She said that she couldn't bear the thought of you having to live on after her death as a Fallen Angel alone and abandoned. Her words Mal not mine." He added as Mal's eyes widened at this last comment.

"I see." Malchediel laid a hand hesitantly on the others arm. "Was I foolish to think that there could be a happy outcome from a liaison between one of us and a Nephilim? It has never happened before has it?"

Nemamiah gave a sad smile. "Not to my knowledge."

Malchediel nodded, resignation visible in his slumped shoulders. He drew a deep breath, "I will need your help in the next few months Nem. Please have patience with me if I seem moody and morose. I never knew love could be so painful." A faltering smile hovered around his mouth. He cleared his throat and then said, "I assume Raguel wants to see me."

Nemamiah was deeply relieved that Malchediel's anger displayed a few days ago seemed to have run its course. "I told him that Raphael has been treating an injury to one of your wings. I'm not sure if he believed me though."

"Thank you my friend. I don't think I could face questions from him right now." In an instant Nemamiah took Malchediel in his arms hugging him warmly before releasing him. "To have you call me 'friend' is all the thanks I need." The relief was evident on his face. "Do you want me to walk with you to Raguel's office?"

"Yes please... Tell me what sort of mood was he in?"

The interview with Raguel was easier than Malchediel expected. The overseer regarded him across the desk before speaking. "I know something has occurred during your mission but quite frankly I don't want to delve into it too deeply. I am quite aware that your friends are covering up something that they don't want me to know about." When Malchediel didn't respond he went on. "You were right when you said that you were my best Warrior Malchediel. We will class your mission a success." He smiled at the Warrior Angel. That in itself was unusual. "Well done. It's good to have you back."

After Nemamiah had left, Amy sank to her knees in the middle of the living room and wept bitter tears of loss. Less than an hour before, she had been in Malchediel's arms yielding to his kisses and caresses. How could everything change so quickly? She was hurting...Oh how she was hurting. As the enormity of what she had lost sank in she lay down where she was on the floor and curling up into a foetal position cried until her throat ached and her eyes burned. Whispering his name over and over as if by sheer force of will she could make him reappear she eventually gave in to exhaustion and slept where she lay.

The next two days passed by in a blur. She didn't wash or dress. She didn't eat. She occasionally filled glasses with water from the kitchen tap to gulp down thirstily whenever her throat began to burn. At mid-morning on the third day she was roused from an all-consuming stupor by a knock at the front door. "Malchediel?" she uttered realising as she said his name that of course it wouldn't be him. Doors were no barrier to him. She ignored the knock closing her eyes once more. Whoever it was they were not to be 'put off' they knocked again. Amy wearily pulled herself up and walked slowly to the door. She opened it and conscious that she was still wearing her pyjamas peered around it expecting to see Stephen. However standing

"Wotcha!" she said and taking in the puzzled frowns on all three faces asked, "What's up?"

Ralph indicated the black phone with a nod of his head. "Someone tried to ring in, on that phone a little while ago."

"I thought that line was defunct." she said.

"So did we. Unfortunately when I tried to trace the caller, they had withheld their number."

"That's the trouble with the rule that we don't answer incoming calls." She complained.

"You know why that rule is in place Ruby." Doctor Steenbergen said with a sigh. "Our Organisation isn't supposed to exist. We protect our anonymity by ringing callers back; it's just unfortunate that the old phone system doesn't recognise withheld numbers."

Ralph shrugged, "I'd love to know who it was. Who the hell would have that number after all these years?"

"Hey Ruby!" Ilya put in suddenly, "Isn't your new boyfriend a Telecom's Engineer? I bet he would be able to trace that number."

"Oh no you don't." she blustered, "I can't ask him to do that. It's against all the rules. He'd get fired if he was caught."

"Why don't you ask him Rubes?" Ralph suggested. "If he says no, then that's the end of it. We'll just forget about it."

All three stood looking at Ruby waiting for her response.

"You buggers!" she exclaimed, "I haven't known him all that long."

"All the better." Ralph laughed, "He'll want to impress you. Ask him... I bet he'll get the number for you. Just tell him someone has been ringing you and not speaking when you answer. If he's keen on you he'll want to impress you."

"What do you mean? **If** he's keen on me? Of course he's keen on me."

All three laughed at her indignation. After a moment she saw the funny side of the situation and grinned at them. "Okay..." she said, "I'll ask him but if he says 'No' then that's that."

"Good girl." Ralph said as he pushed the black phone to the rear of the desk again. "I'm sure Doctor Steenbergen can be persuaded to add a little bonus to your allowance this month for your troubles." The Doctor raised his eyebrows at the comment but they all noticed the barely suppressed lift at the corners of his mouth.

A few days later Ruby was seen entering the Doctor's office clutching a piece of paper in her hand. Within fifteen minutes he had called a meeting of all senior officers presently on duty. He had asked Ruby who despite her youth was a fully trained Nephilim Officer to stay to hear what he had to say. He waited until everyone had filed into his office before holding up the note that Ruby had handed to him earlier. "I don't know how she did it, but our enterprising Ruby has managed to obtain the name of the telecom subscriber whose phone was used to contact the Organisation a few days ago." He gave the little note a wave before going on. "When I first saw the surname it seemed to ring bells in my head." All eyes were on him waiting for him to divulge the mysterious callers' identity. He drew in a breath, "After looking through our records I realised why the name seemed familiar." He paused before going on, "The name was Bernstein." He watched as some of those present looked to each other in puzzlement. He smiled. "If you are younger than your mid-thirties the name will probably mean nothing to you, but Ralph," he said, "you should recognise it."

Ralph frowned clearly thinking hard. Suddenly his furrowed brow cleared. "My God!" he exclaimed, "Melissa Bernstein!"

The Doctors smile broadened. He turned back to the unenlightened faces in front of him. "Most of you would probably be more familiar with the name Melissa Monkshood." He was gratified to see that all present had indeed heard of Melissa Monkshood. There was instant chatter among those digesting the news. A tall blonde girl standing just inside the doorway chipped in. "She died years ago didn't she?"

The Doctor's face took on a sombre expression. "Yes she died in mysterious circumstances, you're right Charlotte. Her husband Roger Bernstein died two or three years ago as I recall."

"So if they're both dead whose name is on the note?" she persisted.

The Doctor looked at the name once again. Without looking up he said, "Roger and Melissa had one child, a daughter...they called her Amy. The name on the note is Amy Bernstein."

There was a general buzz of conversation at his revelation. He spoke up, "It seems that Melissa's daughter Amy has tried to contact us." He turned to Ruby standing right in front of him. "She must be about your age Ruby. How would you like a trip down to Cornwall?"

Chapter One

After Nemamiah had left her, Amy let out a low moan of anguish. Sinking down onto the floor of the living room she gave vent to her tears. Pitiful sobs racked her body. Every once in a while the name Malchediel would escape her lips as she rocked backwards and forwards in her misery. She knew that in all probability she would never see him again. His last words to her were that he loved her and always would. That should have given her hope that he would attempt to escape his captors and come back to her but she had, by her own hand, smashed that hope. Before he left, Nemamiah had made her see how futile was the notion that she and Malchediel could ever contemplate any sort of relationship together. He was an Angel and she a Nephilim, part Angel and part Human. He could pass from his home in Heaven to Earth easily. She would always be bound to Earth. To be together he would have to relinquish his Celestial heritage, turning his back on everything he had ever known. Nemamiah had made it quite clear that such a choice would result in his being banished to live out the rest of eternity as a Fallen Angel. As a Nephilim her lifespan was the same as a Human…she would age and eventually die leaving him alone without the companionship of his kind. She loved him too much to condemn him to such a fate. Before Nemamiah and his comrades had appeared to take him back by force, Mal and Amy had discussed his abandoning his Heavenly home to be with her. It had seemed so easy when he had said that it was what he wanted. Nemamiah had made her see sense. It had been an impossible dream…nothing more, and so she had made the heart-breaking decision to send a message to Malchediel that she wished to end their doomed relationship freeing him to continue in his role as a loyal Warrior Angel. She couldn't bear to contemplate the alternative, to have him branded as a renegade Fallen Angel.

Nemamiah had left her, taking with him the feather that Malchediel had given her when he had declared his love for her. She knew that when Mal saw the returned feather he would understand the message behind it. He had plucked it from his own wing telling her that if she ever wanted him, she only had to snap the shaft and he would be aware of it, "If ever you should need me, I will know ...I will come." He had said handing it to her. Once it was back in his possession he would know that she would never call upon him...ever.

Now alone, her heart breaking, she cried for what might have been. Eventually there were no more tears to shed. Her throat ached, her eyes stung. She lowered herself until she was lying in a foetal position on the floor and slept.

The knock at the door roused her momentarily; her first thoughts were that it may have been Malchediel. Then reason asserted itself. Of course it couldn't be him; he would not have bothered knocking. He would have passed through the door as if it were tissue paper. An Angel didn't recognise walls or doors as barriers. She tried to ignore it but the caller knocked again. She would have to answer...get rid of them as quickly as possible.

The caller was a girl of similar age to Amy with short dark hair. Amy's quick glance took in the several gold earrings that adorned the complete rim of her right ear. Amy scowled at her, "Whatever you're selling... I'm not interested." Surprisingly, the girl didn't seem offended. She smiled broadly, tugging at her shoulder bag. "That's okay, I'm not selling anything." She answered. Amy sighed loudly not really listening to what the girl said next and hoping that her exaggerated indifference would embarrass the girl into leaving. Before she realised what was happening a business card was pushed into her hand. "Look I'm not even dressed yet. I'm not feeling too good." She looked at the card with little interest until her eyes focussed on the bold lettering at the top... **N.F.F.O.** Her eyes snapped up to the girl's face as she proceeded to introduce herself. "Nephilim Fighting Force Officer Shoreditch…Pleased to meet you. May I come in?"

Open mouthed Amy stepped aside allowing her visitor to walk past her into the hallway. As she closed the door she tried to recall what Ruby had said before handing her the card, something about being difficult to track down.

"What do you mean; I was difficult to track down. How do you know me?"

Before she answered Ruby pointed to the door on the left, "this way?" she asked. Amy nodded indicating the living room. Ruby walked through speaking over her shoulder. "You rang our headquarters recently. We tried to trace your number but you must be ex-directory." She walked over to the sofa, "May I?" she asked and when Amy nodded again, she sat down placing her shoulder bag next to her. "The Organisation has a policy never to answer a ringing phone. We guard our anonymity. We always return in-coming calls. That way we can filter out any crank calls or more importantly any 'tracers.'"

"Tracers?"

"Yeah. You'd be surprised how often the other side try to locate our whereabouts."

Amy pinched the bridge of her nose in consternation. "I have no idea what you're talking about." she said. "Look…I'm sorry if I appear a little thick but I only found out about your 'Organisation' recently." Using both hands she emphasised the word 'Organisation' with speech marks. "In fact I also only discovered that I was a Nephilim a few weeks ago. My life has been chaotic ever since."

Ruby smiled broadly. "We figured that your heritage had been kept from you since your mother died. It was noted that both you and your father had fallen off the radar over the last fifteen years or so."

Amy shook her head in disbelief. "You seem to know an awful lot about me which puts me at quite a disadvantage. I only know what Mal…" she stopped herself before revealing Malchediel's identity. "What a friend told me about your lot."

Ruby laughed at her description of the Nephilim Organisation. "Be under no illusion Amy, you are part of 'our lot' too." She looked at Amy noting her pale complexion. "I'm sorry...you said that you weren't feeling very well...is it flu or something? You look pale..." she stopped speaking suddenly as a tear slowly welled up and slipped down Amy's cheek. Ruby wasn't to know that supressing Malchediel's name had caused Amy's heart to plummet down somewhere near her stomach. She dashed the tear away quickly and turned away from Ruby. An awkward silence ensued. After a moment Amy, without looking up spoke again. "I'm sorry..." she cleared her throat before going on, "I'm not unwell...that was a fib. I've had a bit of an upset." She dashed another tear away. "The truth is I have broken up with someone I care about."

There was a pause before Ruby uttered three words, "Ohh I see." She reached across and placed her hand over Amy's...a small act of comfort but it resulted in Amy bursting into tears. Ruby wasn't in the least perturbed by Amy's distress; she waited holding her hand until the flow turned into a trickle. After a while she asked, "Do you want to talk about it?"

Ruby proved to be a good listener but of course Amy couldn't divulge the truth about Malchediel. She gave a very much modified version of the relationship that had developed between her and the Warrior Angel allowing Ruby to believe that he had been a normal human male. She ended with, "We both knew there were considerable differences between us that resulted in our parting ways." She glanced up at Ruby's sympathetic face adding, "It was the sensible thing to do but I did care for him very much and..." she bit her bottom lip to stop it quivering, "it hurts." She looked back down at her hand still covered by Ruby's. Ruby sighed giving her hand an understanding squeeze.

The silence between them lengthened until Ruby ventured asking, "Had this anything to do with you trying to contact the Organisation?"

Amy straightened her shoulders glad that they had moved onto a different topic. "Not really." She said, "I had found out that my mother had been a member of the N.F.F. and someone – a friend – had shown me her original membership card giving the telephone number which I rang out of curiosity.

"Ahh, right," Ruby acknowledged, "That particular number has been replaced although it was never disconnected. When we tried to return your call your number came up as withheld."

Amy nodded, "Yes dad went ex-directory years ago...so how did you find me then?"

"Let's just say we have ways and means but it took a little while." Ruby too was cautious about how much to divulge about her less than lawful means of obtaining withheld telephone numbers. She grinned at Amy. It was at this point that Amy's stomach gave a very audible rumble. Ruby's grin turned into a chuckle. "Haven't you had breakfast yet?"

Amy smiled sheepishly in return. "I haven't eaten for a few days. In fact I haven't done much of anything since Mal left...it's all been pretty much of a mess..." she finished off lamely.

Ruby pursed her lips as she patted Amy's hand briskly, "Bloody men, can't live with them...can't live without them. Look..." she said standing up. "Go get showered and dressed, I'll sort out some breakfast then I can tell you all about the N.F.F."

Going against all her natural inclinations, Amy knew that although she had only met this girl a short while ago she felt she could trust her not to run off with the family silver whilst she was upstairs. She liked Ruby despite her initial irritation when she had opened her door to her. "Okay," she said. "The kitchen is through there.

By the time Amy came back downstairs Ruby was plating up scrambled eggs on toast. She had found the teapot and that too sat on the kitchen table with the promise of the first hot drink for three days. "I hope you don't mind but I left home early this morning and I can't eat anything first thing so I've made enough for two."

Amy eyed the mound of eggs hungrily. "I'm glad you did. It's embarrassing eating alone while someone looks on."

"That's okay then." Ruby said with a smile as she pulled out a chair.

By the time they had eaten their fill Ruby had enlightened Amy about how the Nephilim Fighting Force operated. It seemed that the Organisation was world-wide. Each country operated its network independently but always sharing information whenever necessary. Amy placed her fork down on the empty plate and looked over at Ruby, "How come no-one knows about a world-wide organisation like yours. I had never heard of it until a few weeks ago, and anyway why was it set up in the first place, I mean… a secret private army to fight Fallen Angels…it's like something out of a science fiction novel."

Ruby smiled. "You really had no idea about us? And yet your own mother was a legend within the organisation."

"Ruby, I didn't even know what a Nephilim was let alone that I was one myself. You would not believe what I have had to digest over the past few weeks."

It was then that Ruby asked the question that Amy had no idea how to answer. "So how did you find out about yourself then?"

Amy dropped her gaze from the other girl's face. A part of her wanted to tell Ruby everything but she had only met her a little over an hour ago and how do you tell a stranger that the man you love is an Angel…a real Angel complete with wings and that he had been sent to protect you from another Angel…one who had fallen from grace and was out to kill you. It was bizarre. Who would believe such a story? "Can I ask you something before I answer that question?"

Ruby nodded, "Of course."

"What is your special talent?"

"Sorry?"

"As a Nephilim…what special power do you possess?"

"Oh I see…I'm still trying to perfect it, but my ability is making people see me as someone different, perhaps someone they know. How you see me now is what I normally look like. I'm getting better at it, the more I practice. I can keep it up for just over ten minutes now but it's pretty exhausting. Doctor Steenbergen says that the more I practice the better and easier it will become." What is your special 'talent' as you call it? What can you do?"

Amy took a deep breath, "I only found out recently that I was able to see into people's minds and detect what their worst fear is."

"Ah, okay." Ruby seemed unimpressed. "Anything else?"

"Yes…I can act on that fear and make it happen."

Ruby stared at her. The silence lengthened between them. "Would you like to expand on that?" she said eventually. "Telepathy is a fairly common trait in Nephilim but I've never heard of anyone who can actually exploit someone's fears."

Amy was again unsure of how much to divulge. Ruby had an uncanny knack of asking awkward questions. She decided to skirt over the question with a lie. "I picked up on someone's fear of spiders and conjured a couple of large ones." She said.

Ruby spluttered on the tea that she had been sipping and laughed. "Wow! I must remember to stay on the right side of you from now on."

Amy smiled at the comment but her mind instantly picked up on Ruby's remark, 'from now on.' She had up till this point imagined that this would be a one-off visit but it seemed that Ruby's intentions were more long term. So far Ruby had been asking most of the questions; it was time Amy found out about the secret Organisation that her mother had once belonged to. "Are you allowed to tell me anything about the work you are involved in? It seemed to play a big part in my mother's life. My dad kept our Nephilim background from me after Mum died. I'm only now learning that he did so out of fear for my safety."

Ruby looked at her with some sympathy. "Crikey! I can't imagine how difficult it must be for you to suddenly find out that you're not a normal human. I've had years to get used to what I am and it still sometimes overwhelms me. Because you are from a long line of Nephilim, the Doctor has sanctioned that I can tell you anything that you want to know about our work." She looked steadily at Amy, "He was a great admirer of your mother." She paused giving time for the comment to sink in. "She was quite famous you know. I of course never knew her but her name is well known to all of us."

Amy looked wistful, "That's exactly what I have been told by a friend's father who knew her. I wish I could remember her but I was very young when she died."

"This friend..." Ruby ventured, "I gather he is a Nephilim too."

"Yes, but he is not an active member of your organisation. He and his family try to live as normal humans."

"Very wise." Ruby smiled. "Don't get me wrong. I wouldn't change my lifestyle but it can get a bit hairy sometimes."

Amy looked at her with renewed interest. "Have you ever had any involvement with Fallen Angels then?"

"I've never actually come across any Angels but I've certainly had my fair share of smelly demons. They keep popping up all over the place. It's a good thing humans can't see them, there would be panic everywhere." She paused, "Have you ever seen one?" she asked suddenly.

Amy swallowed. What would Ruby say if she were to learn that not too long ago her home had been invaded by not only a gaggle of Goblins hell-bent on her death but also one of the most powerful of the Fallen Angels... Asmodeus.

"You have seen one! I can tell." Ruby exclaimed. "What happened?"

business…I…um I suppose I've been too busy to think about it…" she finished off lamely.

Ruby laughed heartily, "I'm not talking about undying love Amy. I'm talking about sex! You know fun and games, what makes the world go around. What about this Stephen you mentioned…no bedroom athletics going on there?"

Amy looked sideways at Ruby. As their eyes met they both burst out laughing.

It was a few seconds before Amy realised that this was the first time she had laughed since Malchediel had been torn away from her three days earlier. Ruby was aware that he had been re-claimed by three of his comrades when he had failed to return voluntarily. Amy however had not explained that had they not taken him when they did he would have joined the ranks of the Fallen. He was on the verge of embarking on an affair with Amy, something totally forbidden within the Angelic world. It hadn't happened so why taint his reputation with what may have been.

She didn't want to think about Malchediel. It was too painful. Thinking about him made her heart ache as though a band was tightening around her chest squeezing out any feelings of wellbeing leaving only darkness and despair. She wanted more of Ruby's light-hearted banter. "Do you live at the Manor house where we're heading?" she asked.

Ruby glanced sideways at her, bemused at the sudden change of subject. "I do now. Since Dad re-married I began to feel like an unwanted third party. My step-mother didn't hide the fact that I was an un-necessary addition to the 'Happy Family.' It was better all round for me to move out and the Doctor said I was more than welcome to move in and reside at the hall."

Amy nodded before asking, "Do you feel bitter at the way things worked out…you know…having to move out because your dad re-married?"

Without hesitation Ruby answered, "Nope. Best thing I ever did. I love living there. It's where I have worked since I left school. They trained me in self-defence. They're like a family to me." She paused glancing quickly at Amy again before venturing, "You don't have a family Amy...do you think you might want to move in. It would be great to have another girl living there."

Amy turned to stare at her companion. "Oh...I don't know. This is all a bit sudden. I don't know what to say...Gosh! I just imagined that this would be a two or three day visit. I have a home and business back in Cornwall...it's where I've always lived. You've caught me unprepared for such a decision." She laughed nervously.

Ruby grinned back at her. "Well at least you haven't turned down the suggestion 'out of hand.' We're almost there. Let's see what you think of the place once you've seen it."

Within ten minutes Ruby signalled, slowing down to turn left. She stopped before a pair of ornate iron gates blocking the entrance to a driveway. Amy looked at the polished metal plaque on the pillar to the left. 'St. Alexandra Hall'. Turning her gaze back to the gates she looked beyond them to the tree-lined drive that curved to the right giving no indication of the building that it led to. On the pillar to the right of the gates she saw a remote controlled camera that slowly swivelled to view the car. Ruby wound down the driver's window and leaned out waving at the camera lens. Slowly the gates swung open allowing Ruby to drive through. As she drove on along the cream gravelled driveway Amy looked back watching the gates begin to close behind them. "Security is a little tight I see." She commented.

"You will get used to that Amy. Can you imagine what the popular press would make of an Organisation like ours? We've been around for a long time. We prize our anonymity."

The trees petered out after a hundred yards or so, the drive opening out with wide sweeping views of fields either side dotted with grazing sheep. It was at this point that Amy had her first view of St. Alexandra Hall. It was more modest than she had envisaged. More of a Manor House than a Hall. It was a two storied building fronted by a portico supported by two stout pillars. She noticed several cars parked on the wide expanse of gravel at the front of the building. Ruby swung the car around to the left pulling up next to a highly polished black BMW saloon. As Amy looked towards the front entrance of the house one side of the double front door opened and a small Jack Russell Terrier came bounding out heading for their car barking furiously. Ruby clambered out slapping the front of her thighs and calling out to the little dog. Amy climbed out to stand watching the greeting ritual between the two, a smile on her face. She turned back towards the open front door when she heard the crunch of feet on gravel. Striding towards them was a middle aged grey haired bearded man wearing light coloured slacks and open-necked check shirt. He was smiling broadly in Amy's direction. Ruby stood upright, the little dog still jumping and bouncing around her legs. "Hiya Doc!" she called, moving around the car to stand next to Amy. The Doctor held out his hand to Amy. "No need for introductions I can see you are Melissa's daughter. My God you are so like her." He pumped her hand vigorously, his eyes twinkling with delight. "I'm so glad you decided to visit us Amy."

"I didn't give her much of an opportunity to refuse." Ruby piped up as she unlocked the boot lifting up Amy's case.

Doctor Steenbergen released Amy's hand and took the case from Ruby, leading the way towards the porticoed entrance. "I've put you in the room next to Ruby. I don't suppose you will get much sleep tonight; she can talk the hind legs off a donkey." He chuckled.

Amy smiled but before she could make any comment Ruby had caught her hand and pulled her into the entrance hall heading for the oak staircase that wound its way up to the first floor. Looking up, Amy could see a galleried landing above. Pulling Amy along with her, Ruby skipped up the stairs. On the landing she turned left heading for a thickly carpeted corridor. Four doorways flanked either side. The little Jack Russell terrier was already sitting outside one of the doors his short tail sweeping backwards and forwards across the carpet.

"That's my room." Ruby said. "He sleeps in there with me so I suppose it's his room too." As she opened the door he scooted inside and disappeared from view. She led the way past and opened the next door along. This one is yours then." She stood to one side allowing Amy to walk in. "It's going to be great having you here even if it's only for a few days. I'm still hoping you will want to stay once you get to meet everyone. She bounced herself down onto the bed as Amy looked around taking in the impressive surroundings. "This is lovely." She said wandering over to the window. Looking out she admired the gardens at the rear of the house. "It must be very expensive to run a place like this Ruby. Is the Doctor very rich?"

Ruby stood up and walked over to stand next to her. "He doesn't own this Amy." She laughed. All the properties belong to the organisation…the same as the cars outside." She became aware of Amy's puzzled expression. The organisation is very wealthy. Over the centuries it has accumulated considerable assets much the same as the Catholic Church which is worth millions."

Amy frowned still unclear how a secret organisation dedicated to fighting the forces of evil could have become the wealthy body that Ruby was implying it to be.

"Look…" she started to explain, "All Nephilim families pay dues to the organisation like an income tax even if they are not active members of the N.F.F. When any of us die a further inheritance type tax is levied which also goes into the coffers. It's always been that way. We couldn't exist without that sort of funding. There are also many wealthy Nephilim businessmen who donate throughout their lifetimes. That together with careful investments and other business deals is how we can continue to provide our services to humanity even though they know nothing about it.

"But that hardly seems fair Ruby. It seems as though the Nephilim are all 'give' and the rest of the human race just 'take'.

Ruby laughed. "I like the way you put it, but that's a simplistic viewpoint. Angels were created to protect God's great experiment...mankind. We Nephilim are part Angel which binds us together. We may not have the same powers as the Angels but we can do our part."

"I get that part but what I don't understand is how come we side with the 'good guys' when we were originally the offspring of the bad guys...the Fallen Angels."

"A good point." Ruby grinned, "In fact some Nephilim do fight alongside their paternal ancestors. It's a case of personal choice. Do you want to further your own aims and take the dark path or support the good and do the right thing."

"There's so much I have to learn Ruby. I wish my dad hadn't kept me in the dark about my background. Will I ever get my head around all of this?"

They both turned at a sound from the doorway. The Doctor entered the room with Amy's case. Placing it on the bed he checked his watch. "I'll organise some tea for us. When you have freshened up Amy I'll be waiting in the drawing room. I've been sorting through some old photographs. I'm sure you'd like to see your mum and dad as they were before you were born."

She nodded, "That would be lovely. Thank you." A thought crossed her mind that for the first time since her father had died she felt as though she belonged somewhere...almost like being a part of a family. As the Doctor turned to leave he added, "Ruby, can I see you in my office?"

Once they were left alone Ruby commented, "Men aren't the most subtle creatures are they? I bet he just wants my opinions on what you're like."

Amy lifted one eyebrow, "And what will you tell him?" she asked.

"The truth of course. I'll tell him you're going to be a great addition to the team and you and I are going to be great mates." And with that she flounced out of the room heading for the Doctor's office. Within seconds she was back, "By the way, the drawing room is back downstairs and to the right of the staircase. See you in a bit." She disappeared again leaving Amy to unpack her little case smiling at her new friend's comments.

She hung the few items of clothing that she had bought with her in the wardrobe then explored the door to the left of the bed. It was an en-suite bathroom. Everything that she could possibly require was there. Fluffy white towels draped over a heated towel rail. Bubble bath, soap and shampoo stacked at the end of the bath. This was more like a four star hotel than what she had expected a secret society headquarters to be. But then what had she expected? Military style barracks surrounding a bleak tarmacked squad yard for training purposes? She smiled to herself as she wandered back into the bedroom, beautifully furnished with what must have been carefully chosen antiques. She heard what sounded like motorised machinery from the gardens. She looked out to see someone—a man sitting astride a motorised lawnmower methodically driving up and down the lawns precisely cutting the already (to her mind) neat green sward. *'My God,'* she thought, *'they even have a professional gardener on the team.'*

After she had brushed her teeth and combed her hair she made her way downstairs to the drawing room. She was just about to turn right when one of the other doors leading off the tiled hallway opened and Ruby followed by the Doctor came out.

"Ah, perfect timing Amy." He smiled stepping forward to open the drawing room door allowing the two girls to enter before him. Amy's eyes quickly took in another sumptuous room again overlooking the rear gardens. The drive-on lawnmower had now moved further down the lawns and the noise of the motor was barely discernible. Amy joined Ruby who had chosen to sit on the sofa facing the huge ornate Adam style fireplace. The Doctor took an armchair nearby. Leaning forward he lifted a box file from the side table and placing it on his knees released the clasp revealing dozens of photographs inside. He was just sifting through them when the door opened and a middle-aged woman entered carrying a tray loaded with cups, saucers and silver tea service. The Doctor looked up, "Thank you Marcia ...we'll serve ourselves just leave it on the coffee table if you would."

After rummaging through the top layer of photographs for a few seconds the Doctor lifted the box and carried it over to the sofa, sitting down on the floor between the two girls, "Here we are Amy," he said pulling a handful of snapshots from the box and placing them on Amy's lap. As she started to sift through them Ruby stood up and walked over to the coffee table to pour the tea. The Doctor seeing the vacated seat next to Amy pulled himself up to sit next to her. Whilst she leafed through the photos he kept up a continuous dialogue explaining who each of the characters were and when and where they had been taken. When she reached the first one of her mother she needed no words of explanation. The smiling girl could have been her double. Her eyes drank in her mother's image. She had exactly the same shade of auburn hair as Amy. The Doctor watched her in silence for a few moments then he spoke again. "Can you see your father in the background?" he asked. Amy reluctantly looked past her mother's image to scan the half dozen other figures, her eyes alighting on her father's face. He was standing behind her mother appearing to look at his future wife's profile. The doctor could see that she was clearly moved by the photographs and he quietly stood, walking over to where Ruby was waiting with his cup of tea. Amy continued to look through the rest of the photographs in silence, the Doctor and Ruby quietly talking together in the background.

After about ten minutes she looked up at them, her eyes moist with emotion. She cleared her throat before speaking, "I can't thank you enough. I have so few photographs of my mum." She glanced back down at the box on her lap, "She looks so happy in all of these. I can't remember her at all...I'm glad she was happy." She ended with a sigh.

Ruby came back to the sofa carrying Amy's cup of tea. Amy quickly scooped the photographs back into the box and closed the lid. As she took the cup from Ruby the Doctor suggested that she take the box back to her room before dinner and could go back through them at her leisure.

She smiled her thanks and sipped her tea.

It wasn't long before Doctor Steenbergen broached the subject that Amy knew she couldn't avoid. "Ruby has been telling me something of your involvement with Malchediel. I have in my time had contact with various Angels myself. Unfortunately Malchediel wasn't one of them." He noted the tightening of Amy's lips at the mention of Mal's name and he continued quickly. "Would you care to describe what happened during the incident with Asmodeus? Ruby has given me brief details of his attack but if you feel up to going over it all again I would like to hear it from your lips."

Amy took a deep breath before launching into how she had found out that Asmodeus was probably behind the mysterious deaths of both her parents and how he also wanted her dead because she was the last of the 'Monkshoods.' She explained how he had despised her family since Amy's mother had allegedly caused the death of a former lover of his.

The Doctor shook his head scowling, "I doubt Asmodeus would have batted an eyelid at the death of anyone but himself. He was a cold, vicious being. The only thing he felt strongly about was his own banishment."

"You seem to know an awful lot about him." Amy acknowledged, "I had never heard his name before Malchediel and I met him one day by chance whilst we were out walking."

"Ohh...that wasn't by chance Amy. Asmodeus never left anything to chance. You were meant to meet that day. Tell me what exactly happened and what was said during that meeting."

Amy described how Asmodeus demanded that Malchediel hand her over to him and how he was instantly rebuffed and how he then gave Mal a time limit to comply with his demands. She also told of the sorry plight of the two Guardian Angels who had been sent prior to Malchediel, to safeguard her person. "It appeared that he had tortured one of them by plucking out his flight feathers. "He looked dreadful. Mal sent both of them back to be treated by...I think his name was Raphael."

The Doctor nodded clearly knowing the name of the healing Angel. "Go on...I want to hear what happened when Asmodeus launched his attack on you. Ruby gave me just the brief details."

Amy was just getting to the part where her scream had distracted Malchediel allowing Asmodeus to hurl a javelin at him pinning him to the wall behind him when the housekeeper Marcia returned to collect the tea tray. Amy stopped speaking not knowing whether Marcia was privy to Nephilim business or if indeed she was just an employee. The Doctor took the opportunity to inform the Housekeeper that Amy would be staying for dinner that night and would most likely remain a guest for a few days. "No problem Doctor, I'll set an extra place." She replied as she bustled out with the tea tray.

Amy carried on with her dialogue, the Doctor listening carefully asking the occasional question when something puzzled him. As the room grew darker with the early winter sunset, Ruby quietly went to close the drapes at the three floor to ceiling windows. Before sitting back down in the armchair she switched on the wall and table lamps.

As Amy finished explaining about the bright light invading the bedroom at the moment of Asmodeus's demise the Doctor nodded thoughtfully. "Clearly he was dead at that point." He acknowledged simply. "I have been present at enough Angelic deaths to recognise what you have described."

"I was terribly shocked by what I had done. It was purely instinct after what he had done to Malchediel. I had no idea that I was capable of such an act."

"What you did was of great benefit to Mankind Amy. You have no idea how many Humans, Nephilim and Angels have died at his murderous hands. He was totally void of any compassion, indeed he was motivated only by revenge at being cast out. Be under no illusion, had you not killed him first he would have murdered both you and Malchediel without a moment's hesitation."

"I know." Amy answered quietly, "He made no bones about what he intended to do. I don't regret doing what I did. In fact at the time I was so incensed by his hysterical laughter at the pain he was causing Malchediel; that the only thing on my mind was killing him. It's only now that the enormity of what I did really scares me." She glanced at the Doctor's face, "Does that make sense?" she asked.

"Oh yes Amy. Taking someone's life can have a profound effect on people. Even soldiers during times of war have been known to break down when faced with killing the enemy." He reached for her hand covering it with his own. "Make no mistake we are at war with those Angels that have been banished. It's a war that has been going on for millennia. You just didn't know about it. They are angry. They can't get back at God so they target the human race knowing that He won't just sit back and let it happen. There will always be Angels like Malchediel who will fight for a race that don't even know he and his like exist." He had been looking at her with a deal of gravity as he spoke. Now his face softened towards her. "I think I have interrogated you enough for today Amy. Why don't the two of you go off and explore the house? I'm sure Ruby would love to show you around." He lifted an eyebrow in Ruby's direction.

Ruby jumped up from her armchair, "Good idea, Doc! It's too dark to show you the grounds, we'll do that tomorrow." She skipped over to the sofa. "We'll start with the gym...come on..." The Doctor smiled as the two girls left the drawing room heads together, Ruby already explaining the layout of the house.

The gym was housed in what was clearly a later addition to the house, a wing added on at right angles to the rear. It was very impressive, the training room being fully equipped with every manner of equipment. Ruby showed her the showers and changing rooms next. They made her old school changing rooms look positively archaic. Leading on from there, they approached the gymnasium. They could see lights on through the glass panels of the double doors. "Looks like someone is in there." Ruby mused.

She pushed the doors open and the two girls passed through. There was a single occupant at the far end bouncing a ball as he eyed the basket-ball hoop high up on the end wall. The noise of the ball slamming against the wooden floor echoed around the huge empty gym and the blonde man clearly didn't hear the girls enter from the other end. Ruby placed her finger on her lips indicating Amy to remain quiet as the man took aim and threw the ball. It swivelled around the rim of the hoop and then slid through to bounce a couple of times before being caught by the lone occupant. Ruby immediately began clapping and cheering. The man turned at the sound, a smile lighting up his face. Tucking the ball under one arm he approached them. Ruby and Amy also walked towards him meeting in the middle of the gym. He held out his hand to Amy, "You must be Amy Monkshood?" he said. Amy took the proffered hand. She had immediately picked up on his foreign accent. Ruby made the introductions, "Amy this is Ilya."

"Hello…" Amy responded. "It's actually Bernstein…Amy Bernstein. Monkshood was my mother's name."

"Of course, my mistake. Please forgive me it's just that your mother was a bit of a celebrity within the organisation."

Amy nodded acceptance of his apology taking in his appearance as they shook hands. His hair and the stubble on his chin was very blonde almost white but his eyes by contrast were quite dark. He was slimly built but the biceps exposed by his vest top were well formed. This was someone who regularly trained. There was a slight resemblance to Malchediel although he must have been a good four or five inches shorter. Perhaps it was the blonde hair that gave her a pang of recollection despite to. Turning to the Doctor she asked, "What do you class as a storm? And how do you deal with it when it happens?" She noticed the Doctor glance across at Ilya with a 'Now look what you've started.' expression before laying down his soup spoon. He pursed his lips before looking across at Amy. "I believe the last time we were called to arms was about two years ago. There had been four inexplicable murders in Bristol one evening during December. The police didn't recognise them as murders. All the bodies had been fished out of a canal badly mutilated. The report went out that the four victims, all male, had been out drinking and had ended up drowned in the canal on their way home. The Police thought that one had slipped and fallen in the water and his companions had drowned trying to rescue him. The mutilations were put down to rats having eaten parts of the victims"

Amy had been watching the Doctor as he spoke but then she asked, "Why would you have doubted that? It seems a reasonable assumption."

The Doctor smiled, "But we had already picked up on Demon activity in the area and two of our operatives were sent down to investigate. Sure enough Demon odour was evident all along the canal towpath. Our people only had to wait until the evening to witness more than a dozen of the creatures materialising along the embankment. They just managed to dispatch the lot of them before a canal boat of festive merrymakers chugged into sight. The thought of what could have happened...well...you can imagine..." he trailed off.

"Mal told me about demons and how they can escape from their dimension through anomalies. He said that humans can't see them."

Before the Doctor could make a comment Ilya piped up, "Mal? Who's Mal?"

"Ah we haven't had time to tell you all about Amy's background, have we Ruby?" he smiled.

Ruby who had finished her soup looked smugly at Ilya whose glance went from the Doctor to Amy and finally settled on Ruby for explanation.

"Mal…" she said pausing for effect, "is none other than Malchediel."

Ilya was still holding his soup spoon but his starter was forgotten as he turned astounded eyes on Amy. "You've met Malchediel?" he asked in astonishment.

Amy could feel her cheeks growing warm under his scrutiny. She nodded. "He appeared one morning in my shop in Falmouth a few weeks ago."

Ilya placed his spoon in his bowl no longer interested in finishing his soup. "My God! You've met Malchediel…What's he like?"

What a question? How could she describe the Angel who had casually strolled into her shop on the pretext of viewing her paintings and who had instead stolen her heart. Ruby was instantly aware of Amy's dilemma and took up the story for her. She retold the tale of Amy's first meeting with the Warrior Angel, why he was sent to protect her and how Asmodeus had appeared to extract his own revenge on the last surviving member of the Monkshood family. By the time she had finished, Marcia had cleared away the soup bowls and was now serving the main course of Lamb and vegetables. Amy was thankful for Ruby's stepping in to explain why Malchediel had been sent to protect her from Asmodeus's threat. She hoped that one day she would be able to think about, and speak of Malchediel without feeling the need to resort to floods of tears over what might have been.

The Doctor innocently asked, "Of course now that the threat to your life is over, Malchediel will have returned to his own dimension.

Without looking up from her plate Amy acknowledged his question with a nod of her head.

Once dinner was over the four of them settled themselves in the drawing room where Marcia served coffee. The Doctor and Ilya wandered over to a side table set up in one of the window alcoves to continue a game of chess that Ruby informed Amy had been going on for the past five days. The two girls settled themselves on the sofa far enough away from the men to talk together without being overheard. Ruby sipped her coffee before suggesting quietly, "I know your emotions are feeling bruised and battered at the moment Amy but if and when you want to talk about things I'm here to listen. Amy turned to her new friend taking in her warm brown eyes not twinkling with amusement as usual but full of compassion and sympathy. "Thank you Ruby. I've never had a friend like you before...There are things I want to share with you but not just yet. Give me a little time..." She bit her lip to stop the little tremor that lurked there.

With an acknowledging nod of her head Ruby changed the subject. "Drink your coffee and I'll show you the Control Room before bedtime." she said.

The Control Room was on the first floor. It was more of a suite of rooms really, comprising of a small kitchen area used for making drinks and snacks and a modest bathroom. The control room itself was just that...One end comprising of work units topped with an array of telephones. Amy counted eight altogether. There were several computer monitors that covered work-tops that ran at right angles to the telephone section. A woman in her thirties was sitting in front of a large screen watching a fluorescent green arm moving round in a circular sweeping motion. As she watched, Amy saw a group of possibly ten dots appear each time the arm swept across at a position of two o'clock on the screen. Ruby indicated silence by placing a finger to her lips. As the two girls watched from behind her, the woman spoke, "James...they're to your right about ten feet away. There are nine of them. They're not moving...I think they can possibly hear you. You need to act now James." Amy realised at this point that the woman was wearing headphones and she was talking into a small 'bumble bee' mouthpiece that was positioned a few centimetres from her mouth. As she watched the screen Amy saw one of the dots moved quickly away from the rest of the group. Within a few seconds each of the group disappeared from the screen one by one eventually leaving just the one lone indicator as the arm swept past once...twice. The woman let out the breath she had been holding. "That's it James. Well done. There is nothing showing now. Could you see what they were?"

She listened. Clearly someone was talking to her through the earphones. Amy guessed it was James. The woman nodded to the comments she was hearing. "Okay James, I'll pass that on to the Doctor. Once you've scanned the area, you may as well call it a night... Good work." She slipped the headphones from her ears leaving them dangling around her neck and turned to the two girls standing in silence behind her.

"Hi Charlotte." Ruby said with a smile, "This is Amy...Amy Bernstein." Turning to Amy she added, "Amy this is Charlotte one of our operatives."

Amy stepped forward to shake Charlotte's hand. As the two murmured greetings to each other Ruby went on, "Did James see what they were before he dispatched them."

"Goblins, apparently. James was hoping for something a bit more exciting." Charlotte laughed. She turned back to Amy who was still staring at the screen and the one lone dot that was slowly moving away. She turned her gaze back to Charlotte who was watching her with a smile on her face. "A little mind-blowing when you see it for the first time isn't it?" she commented.

Amy returned the smile, "You can say that again. Did I just see him kill half a dozen Goblins single handed?"

Charlotte laughed, "Nine actually...but he is one of our best operatives."

"I remember the first time I saw a Goblin. It terrified me."

"Ohh, they look worse than they are. They're fairly stupid low life forms. Not much of a challenge unless they catch you unawares. Demons are the really scary enemies. They're cunning. They always do what you least expect."

"Amy's going to be staying with us for a few days." Ruby put in, "I'm just showing her around."

Charlotte smiled. "The Doc hasn't stopped smiling since he found out about you Amy. He keeps coming out with little anecdotes about your mother. He must have been her number one fan."

"I was only small when she died. I can't remember anything about her but the Doctor has given me a box of old photographs of her. It's going to be interesting going through them when I have time."

At that point they all heard a distant voice coming through Charlotte's earphones. "Oops...sorry, must get back to work...I'll see you around then Amy..." and she turned quickly away adjusting the earphones back in place. Ruby linked her arm through Amy's and leading her back towards the array of phones explained what each one was for. Every phone was a different colour and each one, Ruby informed her was linked to one of the U.K. headquarter bases.

"And that black one at the back is the one that you first contacted us on." She grinned.

After they left the Control Room they headed for Amy's room where they spent an hour chatting about Ruby's life at the Manor. Amy was left in no doubt that her new friend was going to stop at nothing to get her to move in and start training as a Nephilim fighter. There was so much going on in her mind that she wasn't going to commit to anything without considerable thought. For the first time in many days she had been able to forget the trauma of Malchediel's kidnap and her misery at their parting but she wasn't going to be swayed by Ruby's friendship or the glamour of the Manor. She needed to think about what she wanted to do with the rest of her life.

By eleven thirty she was unable to stifle her yawns and Ruby decided to say goodnight and return to her own room.

Amy showered and then climbed into bed. She turned off the bedside lamp and lay on her back in the darkness thinking over the memorable day that was just ending. It wasn't long before her thoughts wandered to Malchediel. She wondered what he was doing now and was he thinking about her too. Had Nemamiah, Paschar and Qaphsiel arrived just an hour later than they had, then it would have been too late to abduct Malchediel back to Heaven. Just another hour would have seen them become lovers and Malchediel would have burned his bridges. He would never have been accepted back. Angels were forbidden from forming relationships with mortals…he would have been banished, branded a Fallen Angel never to return. He had been willing to accept that punishment to be with her but his friends were not so agreeable to that decision. They would save him whatever the cost to their happiness. As she lay thinking about that awful night she couldn't find it in her heart to hate them for what they did. A tear welled up and slipped over her cheek to roll slowly down towards her ear and onto the pillow. He was an Angel and immortal…and he was where he should be. "I love you." She whispered but there was no one to hear. She closed her eyes as another tear rolled across her cheek spreading the damp patch on the pillow.

The next morning as Amy was dressing there was a knock on her door. Within a heartbeat of her calling, "Come in…" Ruby bounced into the room closely followed by the little terrier.

"Wotcha! Good…you're up already. D'you fancy a quick swim before breakfast?" She asked.

Amy looked at her watch, seven forty. "What time is breakfast?" she asked.

No set time. Marcia sets out a Smorgasbord from seven o'clock and clears it away at about ten o'clock. We just help ourselves whenever we're ready."

"What a brilliant idea." She said. "Yes I'd love a swim but I haven't bought a costume."

"No probs...You're about the same size as me. You can borrow one."

The two girls' eyes met and they laughed. "I'll go and sort it out. Back in a jiffy." Ruby said as she skipped out of the room closely followed by the little dog. Within five minutes she was back, two bathing suits draped over her arm and the little terrier still at her heels.

"I never asked you his name." Amy said as she slipped her shoes on.

"He's such a scoundrel...into everything, Ralph kept saying 'Here comes trouble' whenever he saw him. I know it's a daft name but that's what we all now call him...Trouble."

Amy laughed, "I think that's really cute and it suits him...Who's Ralph? I haven't met him yet have I?"

"You will today, he's on duty." Turning to the little dog Ruby called, "C'mon Trouble, you can go outside while we have a swim."

The two girls had the pool to themselves that morning and Amy was beginning to get an understanding of why Ruby was so happy living at the Manor. Who wouldn't want their own private pool to use whenever they wanted? Not only that, but the life style Ruby was leading was certainly attractive. She seemed to want for nothing. There had to be penalties for living like this but in truth she could see no downside as yet.

Ruby was an excellent swimmer, her diving was faultless, something Amy envied. She had never mastered the art of diving and rather than embarrass herself in front of Ruby with her noisy 'splat' of a 'belly flop' she took a running jump at the pool. She disappeared under the water bobbing back up seconds later as though the mere joy of taking a morning swim had gone to her head. Ruby, treading water as she watched her burst out laughing at her friend's exuberant antics.

Amy grinned, "You would have had an even bigger laugh if you had seen me trying to dive.

"Ilya taught me how to dive. We'll get him to teach you too." And with that, Ruby struck off down the pool with Amy trying to keep up.

Later at breakfast Ruby asked Amy about her life in Cornwall and they enjoyed a leisurely hour eating and chatting until they were joined by a man Amy hadn't seen before.

"Ahh…this is Ralph." Ruby explained. Amy looked towards the newcomer, a man perhaps in his mid-thirties with mid brown shoulder length hair tied back in a ponytail. Like Ilya he was fairly tall and his denim shirt pulled taut across his chest gave lie to a muscular build. It seemed that apart from the Doctor who was of slight build these Nephilim fighters clearly trained hard. Even Ruby had the body of an athlete. The thought occurred to her that the Doctor was the 'brains' of the outfit, whilst everyone else she had met was the 'brawn'.

Ralph strode across to the table his hand extended towards Amy. "Hello there." He said taking her hand in his. "You must be Amy. Welcome to the Manor." She was aware of a firm handshake…yes he clearly trained hard. "Has our Ruby been looking after you?" he added smiling over her head towards her companion.

"She's been an excellent guide. This place is quite an eye-opener."

"So…first impressions are favourable then?"

"I've already suggested she join us Ralph…She's thinking about it. She's staying for a few days so I have some more time to work on her."

Ralph quirked an eyebrow, "I don't see how you could refuse then Amy."

Amy was beginning to feel a little pressured. "I only said I would think about it. It's a big commitment. I have a home and a little business back in Cornwall. There's a lot to think about…" she trailed off.

Ralph laughed heartily, "Only kidding Amy. This is something you need to work through yourself. Don't let Ruby here nag you into something you're not sure about. She's just craving some female company. You would think she'd be happy with all us guys at her beck and call…" he ducked as Ruby threw her napkin at him, then still laughing he made his way to the sideboard laid out with food to select his breakfast.

Amy smiled across at Ruby. The longer she stayed here and the more people she met, the easier it seemed that she could fit into this way of life…but then she hadn't yet been called upon to join in with the less attractive side of their world…fighting the forces of evil. Her mother was surely a hard act to follow.

After breakfast Ruby asked Amy if there was anything she wanted to do.

At a loss Amy asked her what would normally be doing adding "I want to find out what sort of life my mother used to live, so just pretend I'm not here and follow a normal day's routine." She suggested.

"Okay…" Ruby smiled, "I often train in the mornings, either in the gym or a jog around the grounds with Trouble." Glancing across the table at Amy she asked, "Do you use a gym or do any sort of keep fit?"

"I'm afraid not." Amy answered sheepishly. "I have to confess I did notice earlier at the pool that you are incredibly toned. Evidently you make good use of the facilities here. I used to occasionally go jogging with dad when he was alive but now-a-days the sum total of my fitness regime is a walk to the Bakery at lunchtime."

Ruby laughed as she stood up from the breakfast table, "Well I won't inflict anything too gruelling on you today. How about a tour of the grounds? We can take Trouble. I bet no-one's bothered walking him while I was away yesterday."

The girls wrapped up in warm coats...the weather had at last turned quite chilly giving every indication of a cold winter to come. On their way across the entrance hall to the front doors the Doctor came out of his office. "Ahh...Good Morning both of you." He said smiling, "Off out?"

"Just thought I'd show Amy around the grounds. Did you want us for anything?"

"No, no you carry on...Are you doing a spell of duty in the control room later?" he added as an afterthought.

"Yeah. I said I would cover for Ilya for an hour or two this afternoon while he has his annual medical."

The Doctor nodded. "Okay Ruby." He turned to Amy, "Perhaps you would like to sit in with Ruby...get some insight on how we monitor things..." he wiggled his fingers indicating *spooky goings on* "and how we detect anything, shall we say, out of the ordinary." To Ruby he added, "I understand there have been some strange fluctuations in the magnetic fields across Europe. We need to keep an eye on that. It may be nothing but it could indicate something about to erupt."

Ruby's eyes lit up. "A bit of action..." she rubbed her hands together in a show of anticipation.

The Doctor gave a little shake of his head as he rolled his eyes at her, then with a benevolent smile carried on across the lobby towards the staircase calling out over his shoulder, "Enjoy your walk girls."

They kept up a fairly brisk pace. It was a cold morning; there was still lingering frost on the grass where it was shaded from the sun by tall hedges and trees. Ruby had bought along a ball that they took turns at throwing for Trouble to fetch and return. After a while he tired of that and instead went sniffing and rummaging amongst the fallen leaves. Ruby and Amy with their hands deep in their pockets carried on walking occasionally waiting for the little dog to catch them up. Amy took the opportunity to question Ruby about her life at the

Manor. She was particularly interested in hearing about the 'training routine' that all the operatives went through to maintain a credible fitness level.

"There is a fitness trainer that comes in every afternoon. We are encouraged to attend at least four sessions a week with him but it's pretty much left up to us when we train with him."

"But there are only three of you living here. What if none of you turn up for a session with this Trainer? It would be a waste of time his coming in wouldn't it?"

"Oh it's not just us that he comes in for." Ruby answered, "There are lots of other operatives that attend his sessions. There are dozens of us that live 'off site' but are still fully trained Nephilim fighters. The training sessions are always fully attended. You'll see yourself this afternoon."

On their return to the Manor, Marcia had laid out an early light lunch for those who were intending to train later that afternoon. They were joined by five other officers, four men and Charlotte who Amy had already met. Ruby made the introductions for those new to Amy, one being the Trainer himself. Amy was beginning to appreciate that this organisation was no amateur bunch of weirdo's playing at war games. They were a dedicated private army committed to fighting an invisible enemy. Invisible, that is, to those they protected. Rather a thankless task Amy thought.

During the training session later that afternoon Amy shadowed the trainer who chatted to her explaining some of his methods as they wandered around the gym coaching those who were participating. The trainer, Jim, was older than Amy had first imagined. He told her that he was retired from active fighting being fifty eight years old but he was in excellent shape having been an active keep fit enthusiast all his adult life. He told her that he remembered her mother very well, "One of my best students…" he recalled affectionately. He turned to look directly at her, "You look very like her Amy." He said.

Chapter Four

Amy's stay at St Alexandra Hall lasted just three days before she told Ruby that she needed to return home. Ruby's face fell at the news, "Ohh Amy I was hoping that you were considering joining us here at the Manor. I've really enjoyed having you here."

Although they had only met a few days ago Amy had grown to really like the gregarious girl who had suddenly turned up on her doorstep and she smiled warmly at her crestfallen expression.

"It's a big decision to make Ruby and I have to think long and hard before committing to such a change of lifestyle. You were bought up knowing that you weren't an ordinary human being. All this…" and she made a sweeping gesture with her hand taking in the entrance hall where they had been standing, "is part of your Nephilim heritage. It's the person you are." She looked fondly at her friend, "I grew up thinking I was just another human being. I'm still coming to terms with who my mother was and the life she led before I was born."

Ruby shrugged accepting Amy's explanation but was still unhappy that she was intending to leave.

"Look…" Amy added, "I haven't said I'm not considering moving up here and joining you but I still need to return home. There are things that I need to sort out. I have a home and a business that I have to take care of. I will keep in touch and I promise that I will seriously consider joining the N.F.F. and…" she paused to give her next statement emphasis, "the fact that I haven't completely ruled it out of the question must give you some indication that with no family ties, being a part of your group does have its attraction."

With that last sentence Ruby's face once again showed hope. Grabbing Amy's hand she squeezed tightly, "Oh Wow! I'll ring you every night just so you don't forget me!" She exclaimed.

At that moment Ralph came down the staircase and Ruby turning to him cried, "Amy's thinking of moving in. At last I'll have some female company."

Amy shook her head in mock exasperation, "I'm **thinking** of it Ralph. There's a lot I have to sort out first."

Ralph's smile was one of understanding as he approached the two girls, "I'm sure there is. Don't let our Rubes pressure you into making a hasty decision, but…" he winked at her, "we're all hoping that you will join us Amy."

Rather than have Ruby make another 'round trip' to Cornwall to take her back home Amy decided to go by train. The Doctor and Ruby accompanied her to the train station and saw her safely on the train waving 'goodbye' until she was out of sight. The journey back to Falmouth gave Amy plenty of time to process her memories of her time at the Manor and by the time the train pulled into the station she was already missing her new friends and wasn't looking forward to returning to her empty lonely cottage. One thing she had to thank Ruby for was breaking the endless cycle of depression that had consumed her after Malchediel had been forcibly removed from her. Ruby had given her a glimpse that there was a life after Mal and she was determined not to slip back into that living hell. He had made no attempt to come back to her. Perhaps once back where he really belonged he had come to see the futility of their relationship. She had been given a lifeline by the N.F.F. Whether she decided to join them or not she also had a life to get on with.

The first thing she did after checking through her mail was to ring Alec to let him know she was back. Ten minutes after ending the call, Stephen was on the phone to her. His father had lost no time in passing on the news that she was back home. She promised to meet him after work at The Falmouth Arms for a drink. He was anxious to hear all her news.

When she told him that she needed to pop into her shop anyway, he said that he would pick her up from there at around six o'clock and they could walk up to the pub together.

She made herself a sandwich for lunch. Unfortunately the milk in the fridge had gone off while she had been away and she made a mental note to pick up some supplies whilst in Falmouth later. She collected her dirty laundry adding it to the washing in her weekend case and loaded the washing machine in the utility room. She glanced across at the easel that had been set up holding one of the unfinished Helford River canvases. She always painted in the utility room because it was easy to wipe away any splashed paint from the tiled floor. After she switched on the machine she wandered over to view the half completed view. She had begun the day-time scene first, leaving the second night-time vista propped against the wall. Both river-scapes were identical; it was just the time of day that differed. Her mind went back to the day she had started sketching the scenes on the river bank. Malchediel had been with her. It was the day he confided to her that he didn't want to return to his Heavenly home. She now stood in front of the canvas no longer seeing it. Her eyes held a blank look picturing his face as she remembered him sitting on the wooden jetty. He had explained to her what would happen to him if he revealed to his superiors that he wanted to leave the only life he had known for millennia. She recalled clearly once again the uncertainty in his beautiful blue eyes as he looked away down the river whilst revealing his doubts to her. She had listened, her heart in her mouth as he explained that to leave would mean his joining the realms of the Fallen but as he turned to face her she felt nothing but hope. She loved him and at last she was aware that he felt the same about her. Their eyes met. He smiled at her but it was a smile full of sadness and uncertainty. He had then stood up and walked over to her easel to view what she had so far sketched leaving her to look pensively down along the river. Coming back to the present, her eyes re-focussed on the canvas in front of her. She sighed and turned back to enter the kitchen.

After she had sent a text Ruby to let her know that she had arrived back safely, she drove in to Falmouth. She picked up some essential groceries before opening up the shop. There were a couple of bills which she tucked into her handbag. Someone had left a message on her answering machine regarding a quote for a commission. She returned their call but it was a waste of time because they wanted a portrait of their pet boxer and she had to explain that she didn't take on portrait work. She was in the process of dusting down the canvases hanging on the back wall when Stephen showed up early for their pre-arranged drink.

There weren't many people in the lounge bar and she settled herself near the welcoming log fire whilst Stephen ordered drinks at the bar. Placing the glasses down in front of her he gave her a beaming smile, "It's nice to have you back...you look great Amy. How did you get on...I've been dying to hear all about it."

She returned his smile knowing full well that she certainly wasn't 'looking great.' She knew that she was looking pale and tired but it was nice of him to lie.

"I'm not sure where to start." She said playing with the stem of her wine glass. "How much do you know about the whole N.F.F. Organisation already?"

He had taken a mouthful of his lager and he lowered his glass to the table before answering her. "Probably not much more than you I suppose. I mean I knew they existed but not having been a part of them they were more of a legend than a reality."

She nodded at his comment. "Well, despite them being more or less a private army operating without the knowledge of the regular armed forces they're all fairly normal people...I mean apart from the fact that they engage in war games with Fallen Angels and supernatural beings."

He broke into a grin at her comment but then surreptitiously looked around the bar to see if anyone could overhear them. "So were you sworn to secrecy or were you blindfolded so that you couldn't find your way back to their stronghold again?" he asked when he was satisfied that no one could overhear them.

She laughed quietly. "You've been reading too many sci-fi novels Steve. They were completely open with me about their activities and I'm sure that I could find my way to their headquarters if I wanted to. Let's face it who would believe me if I tried to explain the goings-on behind the doors of a country manor house? They are quite aware that they operate without the fear of discovery."

He watched her as she lifted her glass taking a sip of wine. "Um...did you learn anything about your Mum while you were there?" he asked.

"Yes. The chap that seems to run the show, he's known as the Doctor, remembers her quite well. She was every bit the celebrity that your dad said she was."

"So..." he said without meeting her eyes, "did they try to recruit you into the Organisation?"

She hesitated, and he turned to look at her already anticipating her answer.

"They have asked me to think about it."

"I bet they did." He said coldly, "And are you? Are you considering it?"

"I don't know Steve..."

He huffed impatiently.

"Don't be like that...I said I would think about it that's all."

He pushed himself back into his seat. "You've changed Amy...since he turned up...you're not the same person." He said crossly.

"If you mean Malchediel, you can say his name, and yes I suppose I have changed. I've learned things about my past that I knew nothing about. It seems that both my parents were murdered and I was attacked by a Fallen Angel…" she drew a sharp breath, Yeah I think you can safely say I'm not the same girl I was six months ago." She looked defiantly at him as he glared back at her.

She made to stand up, "Perhaps this wasn't a good idea Steve. I don't want to argue with you…"

He put his hand out resting it against her arm. "I'm sorry. Don't go." He urged. "I worry about you Amy. It's because of what happened to your Mum and Dad that I have these reservations about the whole Nephilim thing. With Asmodeus dead there is no longer any threat to your life." His hand was still resting lightly on her arm. His fingers tightened squeezing gently, "If you join this band of happy goblin hunters you're putting yourself straight back in the firing line."

Her eyes went from his hand to his face. Their eyes locked for a moment before she started to smile at his description of the Nephilim soldiers that she had come to regard as friends. A laugh began to bubble up from within her and at last he started to smile back at her. "I wonder what Ruby would think about being described as a happy goblin hunter." She said.

He sat back removing his hand from her arm grinning a little sheepishly, "Ruby? Who is Ruby?"

The awkward moment had passed and Amy went on to describe the time she had been away and the people that she had met.

They stayed and had a pub meal together and Stephen didn't make the mistake of voicing his criticism of the N.F.F. or indeed Malchediel again. At ten o'clock he walked her back to her car and they parted company to return to their homes.

It was mid-November and all the shops were gearing up for the festive season. For Amy however this was the quiet time of the year. She wasn't selling anything now so there was no point in opening up the shop. She stayed at home and devoted her time to finishing the two paintings of the Helford River. Working on her own gave her plenty of time to contemplate her future. Stephen made no secret of his feelings about her joining the N.F.F. At the same time Ruby rang regularly to check if she had made a decision yet. In early December she suggested Amy come up to the Manor to spend Christmas with them. It was a tempting offer and Amy said she would think about it. Just a week later Ruby turned up at her door. The two girls greeted one another warmly. "What on earth are you doing here?" Amy exclaimed as she held her friend at arms-length before hugging her closely again.

"Thought I'd just remind you of our invitation in person in case you forgot."

"As if?" Amy said linking her arm through Ruby's' and leading her through to the living room.

"Well? Are you going to come?"

Amy looked at her friend and smiled. "How could I refuse after you've come all this way?" she said.

Ruby did a gleeful little dance, "Yes! Yes! Yes!" She cried as Amy grinned at her antics.

Ruby stayed at the cottage for a couple of days whilst Amy tidied up loose ends before they both travelled back to Bath. She had a bad habit of leaving sending her Christmas cards until the last moment but as she was going to be away for at least two weeks she was forced to complete the task before she left.

Stephen had started to drop by occasionally after work to visit Amy now that she had closed up the shop for the winter season and it was the evening that Ruby had arrived that he first met her during one of his 'drop-in' visits.

Amy was surprised at how well they got on as they were such different characters but she reasoned that the well-known saying 'opposites attract' was obviously correct. Later that evening after Stephen had left Ruby plied Amy with questions about him until Amy laughingly asked if she 'fancied' him. To her surprise Ruby admitted that she found him rather sexy. At Amy's raised eyebrows she insisted that he was one of the best looking Nephilim boys she had ever met. "Most of 'our kind' that I've come across are either married, too old or too nerdy." She exclaimed. "Is he attached or anything?"

"I thought you were seeing someone at the moment."

"Ohh…I was but he started to get inquisitive about my background and it was getting awkward having to keep lying. That's the trouble with going out with Sublunaries…things get awkward."

Amy turned a quizzical look on her friend, "Sub what?"

Ruby grinned, "Sublunaries as in Non Nephilim, Non Angelic, ordinary humans."

Amy shook her head at her grinning friend, "My God, I'm learning something new every day. I've never heard that expression before."

"Sublunary…look it up. It's something to do with being an 'Earthling.'" She wiggled her two forefingers to emphasise speech marks on the last word.

The two girls laughed. "It's rather a derogatory term for normal humans isn't it?" Amy suggested.

"Well they haven't got the abilities that we have,   let's face it. Can you imagine their reaction coming face to face with a Goblin?"

"Just as well they can't see them then." mused Amy. "So…" she said picking up on their original conversation, "You are no longer seeing the one you told me about?" she frowned trying to recall the name of Ruby's boyfriend. "He was an Engineer or something…"

"A BT Engineer…yeah…We split up a couple of weeks ago, so I'm footloose and fancy-free again and…" she added, " it would be nice to go out with one of our own kind for a change."

"I see," Amy smiled, "And you think Steve would fit the bill do you?"

"Well you must admit he has the sexiest smile doesn't he?"

Amy cocked an eyebrow but refrained from commenting on Stephen's smile, sexy or otherwise.

Once Amy was satisfied that she had posted all of her Christmas cards and paid any outstanding bills, she visited Stephen and his parents to let them know that she would be away for a few days over the Festive season. She was amused to see that Stephen was as disappointed about not seeing Ruby for a while as she had expected him to react to her own absence. *'So,'* she mused, *'the attraction between the two of them was mutual.'* She actually felt good about it. She had always regarded Steve as a friend but knew that he had harboured stronger feelings for her. Feelings that she would never reciprocate so it was with relief that she watched what could be a budding romance developing.

Two days later the two girls were heading back up to St. Alexandra's Hall for Christmas.

Amy was so glad she had decided to spend Christmas with her new friends at the Hall. From the moment she arrived she had been included in everything that was going on. The men had already felled a seven foot Norway Spruce tree from the Estate and had man-handled it into the entrance hall where she helped Ruby and Marcia to decorate it after it had been positioned near the grand staircase. Marcia had already strung garlands of holly and ivy around the banisters leading up to the first floor. As the three of them stood back to admire their decorative expertise, the Doctor came out of his office to stand with them looking on in admiration.

There were long periods when Amy didn't have time to think about Malchediel at all. It was usually only at night alone in her bed that she allowed herself to think about him. To remember how his eyes would sometimes turn towards her with that heart-melting smile when she was desperately trying to be serious about something. Sometimes he had deliberately misunderstood something she was saying just to get her exasperated only to kiss away her frustration with him. He could be so infuriating but how she had loved him despite his wicked sense of humour. She still missed him terribly but by keeping busy during the day she was exhausted by bedtime which gave little time to dwell on her sadness.

On the twenty third of December there was an influx of guests to the Manor, all of them members of the Nephilim Fighting Force from various parts of the U.K. Amy was asked if she minded doubling up in Ruby's room until Boxing Day evening when the guests were due to leave. Of course both girls were quite happy with these arrangements even though it meant little sleep for either of them as the girl-talk went on late into the night.

Even during the run-up to Christmas all the active members kept up with their training routine and Amy joined in. After the first three or four sessions the aching muscles eased and she even admitted that she was enjoying the exercise.

Christmas itself was one mad round of eating, drinking, party games and good all-round fun. Amy had never enjoyed herself so much before. In the past she had always spent Christmas alone with her father. She couldn't remember what it had been like before her mother had died. She had loved her father but Christmases with him were never like this. She could now appreciate how melancholy he must have been without her mother and how he had tried unsuccessfully to impart a little festivity into the season for her sake. She silently toasted his memory with her dinner wine before returning to the merriment around her.

Later, during Christmas day evening when everyone had drifted off to do their own thing, either reading quietly in the drawing room or watching television in the large lounge Amy sat alone in one of the winged chairs watching the Doctor and Ilya playing chess. She wondered what Malchediel might be doing at that moment wherever he was. Did he ever think about her as she did about him? His last word to her had been, "I love you Amy. I'll always love you." Did he still feel the same way she wondered? The longer time went by without him contacting her, the more she believed that he had accepted that his friends had been right in forcibly dragging him back. Her mind then turned to her own future. What lay ahead for her? Her former life no longer fulfilled her. Malchediel had shown her a formerly unknown world, a dangerous world albeit an exciting one. Could she return to her old life as a talented but unknown artist? She was unsure, but the N.F.F. was offering her another alternative. A chance to use her new found powers. It was very tempting. Perhaps she was her mother's daughter after all. She was deep in thought and only became aware that Doctor Steenbergen was talking to her when in a raised voice he called her name.

"Sorry…What did you say?" she stammered turning towards him. It looked as though he had the upper hand in the game with Ilya who was studying the chess board frowning.

"I was asking if you played chess Amy."

"Very badly I'm afraid." She answered with a smile. "My dad tried to teach me when I was younger but I think I was a big disappointment to him with my lack of skills."

"Ah, we must have a game sometime. Let me see if you are just being modest." He answered lifting his whiskey glass to his lips as he waited for Ilya to make his move.

She repositioned herself in the big armchair tucking her feet underneath her relishing the comfort and the warmth of the drawing room. It dawned on her that the Doctor was fairly certain that she would join the organisation and move to the Hall permanently and as her head nestled comfortably against sight of Ruby and Stephen kissing passionately just inside the porch way. So engrossed were they that they didn't hear or see her. She smiled to herself. At least Ruby was enjoying herself; she wasn't attempting to disentangle herself to hide in the ladies toilet.

The girls set the third of January as the date to return to the Manor. Ruby had been in daily contact with the control room over the New Year period and had been informed that strange occurrences had been detected up and down Britain. Nothing that seemed to arouse suspicion among the populace but definitely cause for concern within the N.F.F.

"There's definitely some sort of link to water." Ruby said as she slipped her mobile phone back into her pocket after the most recent conversation with Ralph. "It seems that we've been detecting heightened electrical activity around parts of the coast and several rivers have burst their banks even though there hasn't been any significant rainfall to speak of." She shook her head frowning before adding, "Ralph says all N.F.F. bases have been put on alert so it's a good job we're going back tomorrow."

"And what does Steve have to say about that?" Amy asked her lips curling into a smile.

Ruby grinned back, "No problems," she said, "He's already said that he'll come up to visit from time to time."

Amy's eyebrows shot up, "You're not planning on recruiting him are you?"

"Nah… He's more a lover than a fighter."

"Ruby!" Amy cried aghast, "You two haven't slept together already have you?"

Ruby didn't answer but her smirk said it all.

Amy laughed. "When did that happen? My God you've been with me nearly all the time. I don't believe you could possibly find the time…or the place." She added chuckling.

"Love will always find a way." Ruby said with a cheeky wink.

Amy shook her head in mock exasperation.

"In answer to your question it was yesterday. Remember when I dropped him off at his house after we took the shop keys back to the Agency so that you could go to the bank before closing time."

Amy nodded recalling how Ruby had offered to call into the Letting Agency leaving her to pay some bills before going home.

"Well..." Ruby went on, "Would you believe it? When we got to Steve's house his Mum and Dad were out." She rolled her eyes adding, "We had the house to ourselves for half an hour didn't we?"

Amy's mouth dropped open in disbelief, then drawing in a breath of astonishment exclaimed, "And you decided to take advantage of the poor chap."

"Poor chap? You've got to be kidding. He's the hottest thing I've come across in a long while." She arched one brow suggestively, "You don't know what you've been missing girl."

Amy flashed her friend a questioning look. "Meaning?"

"Well...on the way to his house he revealed that he had always fancied you even when you were both at school but you had never seemed interested in him. In fact he admitted that he was worried about how you would feel about us seeing one another."

Amy who had been sorting through the clothing that she intended to take with her when they went back to the Manor stopped what she was doing to face Ruby. "I did know that he liked me Ruby but I always thought of him more as a friend." She glanced down at the shirt in her hands adding quietly. "I have never felt romantically inclined towards anyone before Malchediel. I think that's why it knocked me for a six when he came into my life. I'd been out with a few boys. I even slept with one a few times but there was no spark there, so it seemed pointless really. I thought of myself as a bit of a disaster in the bedroom I suppose and I didn't want to repeat it with

Steve. I didn't want to lose his friendship." She looked across at Ruby, "Does that make sense to you?"

Ruby for once was serious, listening to Amy's confession. "Of course. And I'm sorry it didn't work out with Malchediel although I have to say you did aim rather high didn't you...I mean... an Angel."

Their eyes locked for a moment before Amy saw the funny side of the comment and smiled initiating a responding smile from her friend. "Yes, I suppose I did didn't I? Anyway..." she added briskly "You can tell Steve that I am pleased for you both and he has no need to feel awkward about transferring his affections from me to you."

Ruby laughed. "I'll tell him when I see him tonight."

"Ah...so there will be some passionate goodbye's going on later then?"

"You bet!" was Ruby's amused response.

Once back at the Manor, Amy's training began in earnest. To her surprise it wasn't restricted to Physical exercise alone. There were regular classroom lectures covering the whole concept of what being a Nephilim entailed. This was the part of her training that she enjoyed the most and not only because she got to sit still allowing her aching muscles some respite from the torture they were undergoing. These lectures were heavily subscribed to by day students, many of whom were much younger than her. She was now realising just how little she knew about her background. She was learning along with boys and girls of school age. Youngsters who would likely become soldiers within the Force in the future. She found that she was regarded as a bit of a celebrity when it became known that her mother was Melissa Monkshood. Some of the students were beginning to acknowledge their particular strengths and abilities but none had come across as possessing the skill that she had of delving into the very soul of an adversary to detect what their particular fear was. She was surprised when during one of these lessons the Doctor pulled her out before the rest of the class to demonstrate her skill.

"Okay Amy," he said, "Would you care to choose one of your fellow students to illustrate what it is that you can do?"

She looked around at the dozen or so expectant faces all focussed on her. She could feel a rising panic at being suddenly the focal point of all the eyes in the room. Slowly her mind bought forth Malchediel's image when he had been instructing her during the early days of their relationship and she remembered how satisfying it was when she first beheld his aura. He had at that point commented that she clearly possessed talents that she had no knowledge of.

Closing her eyes she calmed herself telling herself that she could do this. She opened her eyes taking in all the expectant faces before her. Her eyes swept the room before alighting on the face of a teenage boy sitting near the back. He blinked a couple of times under her scrutiny. Suddenly he was no longer sitting at his desk but was staring at his arm, a look of horror on his face. He was holding his arm straight out in front of him and he was rigid with fear. Amy knew that what she was seeing was only in her mind and to everyone else in the room the boy was still sitting at the desk looking expectantly at her face. Instantly she knew that his fear was of bees and in her mind he was staring at the manifestation of one on his arm. Without even thinking about it, Amy sent a telepathic message to the boy that there was indeed a bee on his arm. Without warning the boy shot up out of his seat knocking the chair over. He was shaking his arm vigorously attempting to dislodge the invisible bee. The girl next to him shrieked in confusion not knowing what was going on. The boy had leaped a good two foot away from his desk and was now brushing forcefully at his sleeve with the back of his hand. After a moment or two he realised that there was nothing there and sheepishly looked around at all the astounded faces turned towards him. "Um...um..." he stammered as one and then another of the students started tittering at his antics. Within seconds the whole class erupted into howls of laughter. Fortunately the boy saw the funny side and as he bent to pick up the toppled chair he grinned at Amy showing that he held no malice against her for her little piece of telepathic trickery.

After Amy had returned to her seat the Doctor thanked the boy called Dominic for being such a 'good sport' and went on to explain to the class how Amy had come to be aware of her special ability to detect someone's fear and then to work on manifesting it into a reality. The students listened enthralled to the Doctor's description of how Amy had turned the tables on none other than the infamous Fallen Angel Asmodeus when he had launched an attack upon her and Malchediel the Warrior Angel who was acting as her Guardian. "Up until that time Amy had no idea that she possessed such an ability and it without a doubt saved the lives of both Malchediel and herself. For myself I have never come across this talent before and I am sure that we will be calling upon it regularly now that Amy has agreed to join the N.F.F."

Amy could feel her cheeks growing warm under the admiring gazes of the other students and was beginning to think that even the punishing physical training was preferable to this.

Chapter Six

Malchediel and his team were kept busy over the following months. There was no let-up in the pressure being mounted by the Fallen. If anything they were stepping up their sporadic attacks on Earth. The team hadn't seen this level of assault for centuries. It was disquieting, was it building to something big? The attacks were inconsistent and global as though the Heavenly force were being tested. Their strength assessed and their speed of response gauged. All the teams of Warrior Angels, and there were many, were keeping a lid on it but in the past, attacks had been fewer and localised to particular areas wherever an anomaly had opened up between Earth and the underworld.

Raguel gathered all the teams that weren't out on operations one day to discuss his concerns. It appeared that the Fallen Angels had discovered ways of opening up portals in areas where they had previously been unable to materialise. These new openings it seemed were located near water. Had they discovered a way of harnessing the power of hydrodynamics? It was worrying. Two thirds of the Earth's surface was covered by water. If the powers of evil had found a way of using that element for their means, the results could be catastrophic. Raguel instructed his teams of Warriors to be vigilant and report any strange happening immediately.

Malchediel's team had been out on a mission at the time of Raguel's meeting but Orifiel passed on the overseer's comments on their return. Malchediel's first thoughts centred on the county of Cornwall, that narrow finger of land completely surrounded by water. Cornwall...where Amy lived.

It shocked him how her safety was the first thing that entered his mind on hearing Orifiel's news. He had spent months trying to push all thoughts of her to the back of his mind. He believed he had succeeded but at the first hint of danger, she was all he could think about.

He spent an anxious night finally steeling himself to asking for an interview with Raguel in the morning. On entering his office he noticed the worried frown and dark shadows beneath Raguel's eyes. Clearly events were weighing heavily upon him. He was poring over maps and schedules strewn across his desk. Without looking up, he spoke, "Yes Malchediel, what is it?"

"I have spoken to Orifiel. He has passed on your concerns about the increase in attacks from the underworld." He waited for a response but Raguel's attention was focussed on a map showing the west coast of the United States of America. Mal went on, "I wondered if I may be allowed to do a quick check on my Nephilim girl?" His heart was thundering in his chest just mentioning her after many months of pushing all thoughts of her away. Raguel still didn't look up at him. He was now pencilling in a heavy red line along the San Andreas Fault, making it stand out starkly. "Hmmm? Why is that Malchediel?" he said at last.

Malchediel drew in a slow breath hoping his next words weren't going to sound as tense as he was feeling. "I just thought it may be a good idea to do a 'follow-up' check on her especially as where she lives is almost an island completely surrounded by water." He could feel a bead of sweat trickling down the side of his face. He must not let Raguel see his anxiety. As casually as he could, he added, "With your concerns about invasion by water perhaps I could assess any risk around the coastline of Britannia while I am there."

Raguel put down his red pencil and at last looked up at Malchediel who stood firm under his overseer's scrutiny. Had he given himself away? Was Raguel going to refuse his request guessing at some underlying ruse for his petition? The seconds ticked by as both Angels faced each other.

"How long do you think it will take you to ascertain this information?"

Malchediel couldn't believe he was actually going to consider his request. As nonchalantly as possible he answered, "A day...maybe two."

"You have three days." Raguel offered without hesitation, "You may be my best Warrior but even you would find it difficult to assess the coastline of Britannia in less than that."

So Raguel thought that his main aim was to report back on possible coastal attacks...well so be it. At least he had permission to go and that was all that mattered.

Nemamiah wasn't so easily fooled when Mal told him of his plans. "I have to ask you this Mal...are you going to see Amy?"

Malchediel's jaw tightened and his eyes flashed angrily before he controlled his temper. "You have no need to worry Nem. I won't be making any contact with her."

They eyed each other both attempting to see more than their words were conveying. Eventually Mal repeated with emphasis, "I won't try to speak to her. She won't even know I'm there."

After a moment's hesitation Nemamiah nodded before turning away.

Malchediel breathed a sigh of relief.

Now that he had gained his overseer's approval to return to Cornwall, Malchediel lost no time in preparing for the journey. He wished he still had his denim jeans but his abduction had been so swift that he had only been wearing underwear at the time. It was winter back on Earth and he only possessed cropped pants. He would probably need to purchase warm clothes when he got there. Although he didn't feel the cold, if he was seen, he would attract attention wearing summer gear in February. He slipped his black debit card into the back pocket of his cargo pants. He stood still deep in thought remembering Amy's startled expression when she had first laid eyes on the shiny unadorned piece of plastic. Pushing the vision away, he turned for the door of his room. He stepped out into the corridor to be met by Nemamiah who had been waiting for him. He pushed himself away from the wall that he had been leaning against. Malchediel scowled at him. He knew Nem wasn't happy about him returning to Cornwall but he hadn't expected to find him waiting outside his door for him.

"**What?**" he said tersely as he made to brush past him.

"Okay, okay, I just wanted to see you before you left."

Malchediel carried on walking leaving Nemamiah to scoot after him.

"Why? Thinking of trying to talk me out of going?"

"No...no I was going to ask if you wanted me to accompany you?" Nemamiah's voice held a note of trepidation.

Malchediel spun round so quickly Nemamiah almost ran into him. "By all the saints Nem!" he clamped his lips shut staring at his companion in agitation, He took two deep calming breaths, "Look Nem...have a little trust in me. I know what all this is about. I shall only be gone three days and in that time I have to reconnoitre the entire coast of Britannia. Even if I wanted to, which I don't, I won't have time to make contact with Amy." He sighed taking in his friend's worried expression. "I just want to see her briefly just to put my mind at rest that she's alright. I won't let her see me." He reached out and placed a hand on Nememiah's shoulder. "I promise." He couldn't remain angry with his friend. He knew he was doing what he thought was right because he cared about him. He smiled adding, "I'll see you in three days' time." After a brief man-hug he turned and carried on along the corridor leaving Nemamiah to stare after him.

Once outside he removed his shirt and tied it around his waist before standing upright. The muscles in his stomach flexed as he arched his back, pushing his shoulders backwards. Slowly his wings unfurled. He didn't open them fully allowing them to drape down his back. When the tips almost touched the floor he sent two strong pulses through them forcing them to spread to their full extent. He breathed in deeply before bending to push off powerfully from the ground. Within seconds he was high above the complex that housed the accommodation of the Warrior Angels. He circled twice before turning south and with a sudden burst of energy and light disappeared from sight.

He decided to approach from the north-west flying down the west coast from the Outer Hebrides to skirt the rugged coastline past Skye and southwards checking for any anomalies around the Firth of Clyde. There appeared to be nothing unusual so he flew on, moving into the Solway Firth which too gave every indication of normality. Finding nothing to arouse his suspicion he hastened further south paying particular attention to the Mersey estuary. He knew that Raguel was concerned about the Fallen using their powers to instigate flooding of coastal towns. There had to be a reason for their opening up portals in and around water. Major cities like Liverpool and Manchester not to mention the capital London could be extremely vulnerable if water were to become their new chosen weapon. He hung motionless above Liverpool scanning the scene below. A slow downward beat of his wings kept him steady as he used his senses to detect anything unusual. The air rising from the metropolis below was charged with electrical energy, something he needed to report back on his return. It could be nothing but it needed further analysis. Satisfied that there was nothing of immediate concern he carried on westward flying through the Menai Straits and on down the broad sweep of Cardigan Bay. The area was sparsely populated so he flew on. The next area that he wanted to check out was the south coast of the principality of Wales. The Bristol Channel between Cardiff and Bristol could be problematic if the Fallen chose to instigate a Tsunami. It had happened in that area before when a moderate Tsunami swept up the narrow channel flooding land on either side. That had been a natural disaster. Tidal flooding caused by Celestial forces would be catastrophic. Again he hovered above trying to detect any evil presence. Once satisfied that all appeared normal he swept back westward to follow the coastline of Devon and finally Cornwall. He had been telling himself that this was just a reconnoitring mission but the closer he came to Falmouth the faster his heart began to beat. By the time he swung around the Lizard Point he could almost feel it through the muscles of his neck. For over three months he had given every impression that Amy was a brief encounter in the past. Who was he kidding? Just being in the same area as her, had all his senses tingling. As he approached the little coastal town he remembered to switch to a state of invisibility. It was broad daylight and if he were to land it would probably be in the town itself. His outline shimmered, paled and he vanished from sight. Only a Nephilim would be able to see him now and as far as he knew, apart from Amy, there was only one Nephilim family living in Falmouth. Slowly he came down at the harbour, the downdraught of his wings stirring up dust and leaves around him. An elderly woman oblivious of his presence stopped to adjust her coat collar, pulling it up tight under her chin as she scowled at the sudden windy blast. Normally Malchediel would have grinned at being the cause of her consternation but now he had other things on his mind. He headed up the short hill to the main street and turned right heading for Amy's shop. He had to be careful, she was a Nephilim so would be able to see him, He stayed on the right hand side of the main street opposite her shop ready to dodge into a doorway if she or Stephen her Nephilim friend should happen to be around. As he drew closer he detected that the shop appeared to be in darkness. It was a winter's day and although only early afternoon every shop that he could see had the interior lights on. He approached steadily, glancing around as he walked closer. There was definitely no sign of life from within and as he came to a halt directly across the road from her doorway with a sinking heart he could see the 'closed' sign hanging within. He uttered an expletive. All this way, he longed to see her and she wasn't at the shop. He had to see her. He couldn't return without seeing her. Turning on his heel he comment to Ruby would cause her friend to appear as that particular entity. Her transformations were real enough to cause a myriad of reactions amongst the students.

During April the weather turned severe. The usual Spring April showers were replaced by torrential downpours that lasted for hours. Day after day the deluge continued the length and breadth of the U.K. Over in East Africa the Spring rains did not subside as they usually did. The world's meteorological experts reported higher than usual rain across the Globe. Only the N.F.F. guessed that this was not just freakish weather patterns. This was being created by the army of the Fallen. They had waited for millennia to be forgiven past trespasses and be allowed to return to their Celestial birthplace and were now realising that there would be no clemency for those who had defied the Creator. They now realised that their banishment was permanent and their fury at this knowledge knew no bounds. They had nothing to lose and were now hell-bent on revenge for what they had lost. The battleground had moved from Heaven and that suited them. What better revenge than to cause death and destruction upon the Creator's big experiment...Mankind.

Day after day it continued to rain and at night there were thunderstorms the likes of which had not been seen before particularly so early in the year. The human population talked incessantly about Global warming. This was what happened when Governments failed to stop the destruction of the rain forests and humanity failed to curb the emissions of greenhouse gasses...Oh the fools had got it all wrong but then who still believed in Angels these days. Everyone looked to science to explain what was happening and so no-one was tackling the problem at its source.

Many fishing vessels were lost in heavy weather. There had always been accidents at sea and fishermen occasionally drowned, it went with the territory but never on this scale. No-one questioned reports following the capsizing of a small

Mexican fishing boat. Of the six man crew, fortunately only one had been lost. Mexican television showed the five remaining men excitedly telling of a team of Angels plucking them from what would have been a watery grave to carry them by wing to safety on land. Their story was put down to hysteria born of their Catholic up-bringing and it only made news in Mexico. In truth most of the Angelic host were working tirelessly trying to combat what the Fallen had set in motion. Malchediel and his team was only one small band that was involved in working behind the scenes to try to prevent the next disaster.

The Fallen Angels of which there were several thousand all had the ability to conjure their own Goblins and Demons and it was these creatures that were used in the front line of attack. They were expendable and easily replaced. Now that Lucifer and his Generals had declared all-out war, these low life forms, invisible to humans were bought forth from the underworld to maim and kill at will, leaving the Fallen Angels to pool their powers creating the crippling storms across the Globe.

People were regularly being swept away in rivers and along the coastlines. There were countless deaths caused by falling trees and masonry from buildings. Power lines were cut, trains derailed, planes forced down and even a passenger liner sank with the loss of over a thousand lives.

The newspapers were having a field-day and still no one suspected who or what was behind it all.

It was amid this chaos that the Doctor called an emergency meeting one morning in late April. Word had been sent out the day before for everyone available to present themselves at the Manor by ten o'clock the following morning. By nine thirty there were already more than one hundred Nephilim officers crowded into the board room, the only room big enough to hold them all.

At a little after ten o'clock the Doctor entered the room followed by Ralph and Ilya. The throng of people parted allowing the trio to walk to the centre of the room. Speaking loudly so that all would be able to hear him the Doctor began.

"You are all well aware by now that we face the biggest threat to our way of life that has ever confronted us." As he spoke he turned his head so that he was able to address every-one around him. "Mankind has endured many wars before and has survived. Terrible wars where cruelty seemed to know no bounds, but…" he paused to give his next word emphasis, "They were fought by man against man. What we face this time will be like nothing we have endured before. This time…" he turned once again so that those behind him could see his face, "This time we are up against supernatural powers. This time we will need all our ingenuity, skill and special abilities if we are to survive. The Fallen know that this is make or break time for them also. There can be only one winner in this battle. Make no mistake they want to destroy us. They have nothing to lose. If they can bring the human race to its knees, they will have beaten God…and I believe that this is their aim."

The room was deathly silent. Not every-one present had believed the seriousness of the situation and the Doctor's words had a profound effect on every-one listening. The Doctor went on, "We know that the Fallen Angels are sending their creatures through anomalies from the underworld into our cities. These anomalies are all located around water and we have been monitoring certain areas where they are breaking through. We need to curb this steady flow. Within the next twenty four hours teams of N.F.F. officers will be deployed globally to these points to despatch these minions as they appear. Hopefully this will weaken their fighting force leading to the Fallen to make the decision to show themselves. We are banking on the 'Good Guys' arriving to take over matters at this point." He smiled at the Nephilim around him, "I'm sure you all know who 'the Good Guys' are. The Warrior Angels have always turned up when needed in the past. I'm sure they won't let us down now." There was a ripple of subdued amusement among the listeners at his description of an Angelic force but all present were in no doubt of the seriousness of the situation. At the mention of the term 'Warrior Angels' Amy felt her heart constrict, as memories of one particular Warrior Angel flashed through her mind.

"Good. Looks like we may be seeing some action." Ruby's whisper bought her back to the present. Amy turned to her friend standing at her shoulder.

"Have you ever been involved in anything like this before?" she asked quietly.

"Probably not quite like what's going on at the moment but I have been out hunting as part of a team a few times."

"Hunting? You make it sound like some sort of sport."

Ruby was unable to answer as the Doctor started speaking again. "All of you that are a part of the active team, I would like you to keep your mobiles charged and on hand. You may be called at a moment's notice. Members of the administrative team, would you please see Ralph before you leave this evening to volunteer your services on a Roster system. From now on and for the foreseeable future the Control room will be manned by a two man team."

"Or woman!" came a female voice from the back of the crowd.

The Doctor grinned, "Or woman." He agreed to another ripple of laughter.

Despite ending on a light note, the Doctor headed back to his office in a mood of despondency. He had been in touch with many of his counterparts across Europe and the United States. There had been mixed reaction to the suggestion from the Head of the London organisation that the NFF 'come out' and declare themselves for what they were, an organisation of Nephilim dedicated to maintaining the status quo between the unsuspecting human race and any form of supernatural threat aimed at destabilising their way of life. Doctor Steenbergen had been the head of the South Western organisation for long enough to know that unlike former skirmishes with the Fallen; this time there would be no backing down. This time for the

Fallen, it was all or nothing. For millennia they had endured the stigma of being outcasts, untouchables constantly being refused re-admission to the realm of Heaven and they had had enough. If the Creator repeatedly refused forgiveness then they would attempt to bring Him and his faithful to their knees...or perish in trying. Either way millions of humans would suffer the consequences of a holy war, the like of which planet Earth had not seen before. The Doctor was under no illusion of what Lucifer and his generals were capable of. He was now undecided on the merits of going public with the news that for thousands of years there had been a race of mixed human and angelic beings living alongside and secretly protecting humanity. This was the twenty first century when almost every strange phenomenon could be explained scientifically. The Nephilim race was mentioned in the bible but how many people had ever heard of the term? Indeed most humans, although aware of Angels did not believe they actually existed. What sort of hysteria would be unleashed by claiming that a race of Nephilim possessing very un-human powers had been around throughout history? Back in his office he e-mailed his London counterpart expressing his reservations about going public with the news. It seemed that he was not the only commanding officer wishing to retain anonymity for the organisation and according to Doctor Levinson the present head of the South East division, it had been decided to 'hold fire' on any announcements for the time being.

As the Nephilim and the Angels worked separately and had done so for centuries past, there was no contact between the two but it was universally recognised that the Angelic Host would be aware of everything that was going on and would be monitoring events as they happened. It was therefore no surprise that when the final assault came both parties would join forces to protect the unsuspecting human race from the greatest threat it had ever had to face.

Chapter Eight

It was August. It had been raining almost non-stop for over three weeks. Everyone was thoroughly narked by the weather. Summer holidays had been ruined. Even the tropics had endured the worst down-pours for decades. If only the complaining tourists knew what was in store, the bad weather would have been the least of their worries.

There had been little activity in the area covered by St Alexandra Hall unlike what was being experienced by the other bases around the United Kingdom, the South East in particular. Doctor Levinson had resorted to calling upon other regions to send reinforcements to combat the nightly attacks they were enduring. So far Doctor Steenburgen had maintained his staff intact should attacks step up in his own area as indeed they did during the third week in August. Unknown to Amy, Malchediel and several other teams of Warriors had been involved in skirmishes with groups of demons across the country for several weeks. Unlike the Fallen Angels who were holding back reserving their energies; the Warriors were kept busy despatching demons and goblins by their hundreds in nightly attacks. They knew they were being worn down by the constant onslaught but there was little they could do to reverse the trend. They just hoped that the Fallen would show their hand before too long. This continuous non-stop conflict was draining. The numbers of demons being sent against them was endless and although they were easily eliminated they were quickly replaced by more. They needed to cut off the supply at source and that was only possible when the Fallen themselves joined the battle.

Eventually Doctor Steenburgen's area came under attack. Reinforcements were quickly despatched to the Tamar river valley when the river burst its banks flooding miles of surrounding farmland. A number of people caught unawares by the ferocity of the flooding had drowned and homes had been deemed uninhabitable due to the flood waters. Sewage had escaped into the water system and that just added to the mayhem. A team of Nephilim officers was despatched to the area to combat the threat of Demon activity that was sure to follow. The regular army had also been drafted in to cope with the temporary rehousing of citizens in local community halls around northern Cornwall. Amy, as she was Cornish by birth and knew the County well, was included in the team sent from St Alexandra Hall. What she saw on arrival in the area shocked her. The area had been virtually cut-off from Devon and the rest of Britain. Communication links were tentative at best. Hospitals were barely coping with the influx of the injured. Fresh water was in short supply and was being transported into the county in tankers. Many of the roads into Cornwall had become impassable due to the flooding caused by weeks of rain. The supply of electricity was sporadic and the army had resorted to setting up soup kitchens around the north of the county to supply at least one hot meal a day for the public. The team of Nephilim fighters arrived in a convoy of vehicles during the early evening of Thursday. They had witnessed a steady stream of people trying to get out of Cornwall seeking shelter 'up country.' There was little traffic trying to enter the county itself. They set up residence in the home of a Nephilim family who had turned over their farmhouse and outbuildings to the team before leaving themselves to seek safety and shelter with family members in Hampshire. It took a couple of hours to assemble their tracking equipment in the large kitchen but once set up they began to pick up traces of Demon activity across the flooded area. Ralph, as the senior officer present, formed teams of three of four officers to send out to combat the threat. He would stay at the farmhouse to monitor and direct the teams using the equipment that Amy had first encountered in the control room at their base. Amy was placed with Ilya and another officer who she had occasionally trained with called Mark. Her friend Ruby was in a different team sent to another area along the Tamar valley. Ralph would be able to monitor each team using a radar screen. As the Demons usually worked at night, the teams were instructed to return to the farmhouse around dawn the following day. Amy drew in a deep breath as she clambered into the Land Rover vehicle left by the Farmer for their use. So...the time to use her training had finally arrived.

Meanwhile, the teams of Warrior Angels working in the south east were keeping pace with the Demon activity around the River Thames. They were being kept aware of on-going conflicts around the planet and it gave Malchediel cause for concern to learn of the chaotic events in northern Cornwall. He had no idea where Amy was. She may not even have been in that county at all but the uncertainty was a worry. He had been telling himself for months that she was no longer his concern but he could not deny that he would be re-assured to know that she was in no danger. Why could he not forget the girl? After all she had been the one to cut ties with him. His initial shock and hurt at receiving the returned feather had slowly turned to anger at how quickly she could dismiss him. His last words to her had been his declaration of undying love...how could she be so faithless? So why did he now worry about her safety? But he did. He constantly checked on what was happening on that thin finger of land extending out into the Atlantic.

As it happened his cause for concern it seemed was warranted. The autumn storms that frequently battered the coast of Cornwall came early that year, no doubt with the assistance of the Fallen. Many of the harbours along the Atlantic coast of Cornwall took a severe pounding following days of relentless gale force winds and unnaturally high tides. Of course it wasn't only Britain that was suffering. Japan had declared a state of emergency following freak storms. Tidal waves were battering the east coast of India. Many of the Polynesian islands in the Pacific were now submerged below water with an inestimable loss of life. All this was happening across the Globe but Malchediel, in spite of his inner voice of reason, could not help but focus on what was happening in the south west of Britain.

Ralph had sent a message back to Base for reinforcements. He was picking up on more and more demon activity showing up on radar. There had been several reported incidents of people going missing, their bodies later being found washed up on beaches and river banks. Only the teams of Nephilim knew the real cause of their deaths.

Because of all the Demonic activity going on, there was a deal of confusion surrounding the issuing of orders among the Warrior Angels. Malchediel took advantage of this to deviate from his present instructions to monitor and patrol along the Thames estuary. He communicated telepathically to Nemamiah that he was following a reported sighting of Goblin movement inland and would return once he had investigated the source. With that he headed south west for the town of Falmouth.

He assumed a cloak of invisibility as he hovered above the town. As was normal during heavy fighting, the Angels were in full armour. He was wearing a burnished breastplate, vambraces and greaves and was quite a sight to behold although completely out of place in the main street of the Cornish town. He quickly assumed a cloak of invisibility. As he hovered, he removed his helmet shaking out his hair before descending to land outside Amy's shop. He looked with a sinking heart at the new sign above the doorway, "Books and Brick-a-Brack."

"What in the Saint's names is Brick-a-Brack?" he muttered to himself. Holding his helmet in his left hand he shielded his eyes with his free hand and peered through the window. Inside sat a middle aged woman reading a paperback book. The shop was empty of customers and the woman was clearly passing the time reading. Malchediel stepped backwards uttering an oath. What had happened to Amy's little art shop? Where the hell was she? "Stephen!" he murmured...Stephen would know. He turned quickly heading for the butchers shop along the High Street. There were few people about. It was raining heavily although Malchediel was barely aware of it. He reached the shop he was looking for and stood outside looking through the large glass window. He could smell the joints of meat from where he stood and as a vegetarian he felt his stomach lurch at the offensive odour but he stood his ground. His hair was streaming water down his face and was hanging in matted tendrils over his shoulders, but still he waited not moving. Eventually Stephen who was inside counting out change into a customer's hand, looked up and caught sight of the soaking wet Angel without. Fortunately the elderly woman was looking down as she deposited the coins into her purse and didn't see Stephen stagger back in shock at seeing the one person he thought he would never set eyes upon again. At last she looked up at Stephen and seeing his eyes fixed upon something outside, followed his gaze but of course could see nothing. Had she been able to see what Stephen was looking at with his Nephilim ability to see Angels, she too would have staggered backwards. She quietly said goodbye to Stephen and left the shop raising her umbrella as she walked passed Malchediel who stood motionless staring at Stephen.

"Joe!" Stephen called into the back of the shop, "Mrs Tregenza forgot her sausages...I'll just run after her...okay?" With that he skirted around the counter and headed out of the shop. Malchediel turned as Stephen confronted him taking in his armour dripping with rain water. "What the Hell..." He glanced quickly back through the shop window to see Joe coming from the rear to take over the counter. Stephen grabbed Malchediel by the arm and pulled him towards the alleyway that ran along the side of the shop. Malchediel followed scowling at the manner in which he was being pulled into the alley. Once out of hearing from any passers-by, Stephen turned to face the Angel looking him up and down. "Hellfire! What the hell have you got on? For Christ's sake what are you doing here?"

Malchediel glared back at the youth, "Still blaspheming I see." He said coldly. "In case you hadn't noticed we're at war, but you carry on cutting up dead animals…we'll sort it all out for you."

Stephen blanched at the accusation. "I never played at war games as you are well aware. Not all Nephilim have the stomach to kill at will." He threw back.

The two eyed one another both breathing heavily. Malchediel's jaw tightened, "I haven't the time for this…where is she?"

Stephen hesitated before answering. "If you mean Amy…she left…not long after you abandoned her, you Bastard."

With lightning speed Malchediel grabbed Stephen by the throat slamming him against the alley wall. With a snarl he demanded, "Just tell me where she is boy."

Stephen let out a choked sound and Malchediel released his grip on him. As he massaged his bruised throat Stephen croaked, "She went and joined the merry band of freedom fighters didn't she?" He glared at the Angel, "Before you turned up she led a normal life. We all did…then God's messenger turned up…didn't you." He ceased his ranting breathing heavily. Malchediel was looking at him digesting what had been said. His lips parted but no sound came out. He ran his hand through his bedraggled hair closing his eyes for a moment in frustration. "You mean the N.F.F?" he uttered.

"Yes…I mean the N.F.F." Stephen hissed back.

Malchediel closed his eyes once more, hanging his head. Stephen waited feeling uncomfortable as the seconds stretched out. After a while Malchediel looked back up. As their eyes met once more Stephen sensed that the fight had gone out of the Angel.

"I didn't abandon her. I was forced back against my will."

"Oh yeah…you're here now aren't you…left it long enough didn't you?"

He had referred to her as Officer Bernstein. The acknowledgement had a strange effect on her...Would her mother have been proud of her...would her father have shaken his head in dismay? With a determined stance she answered, "Come on...there's work to be done."

Ilya smiled warmly at her, "Good girl."

After such a close shave to one of the team, Ilya decided to carry on the hunt as a group. He had been impressed with Amy's response when asked if she wanted to carry on but he was well aware that she had been badly shaken. Within fifteen minutes of searching for more Demons, they found them, about twenty of them in a clearing within sound of the sea. They were not alone. Standing a little way from the huddled group was a Fallen Angel who Ilya assumed to be the one who had called them forth through an anomaly which was still gaping behind him. Caught unawares by the three Nephilim before he could usher any more through, he issued a howl of fury. The demons, totally confused, scattered in all directions stumbling over one another with no clear plan of attack or indeed defence. Ilya was the first to fire into the confused mob taking down three almost instantly. Upon seeing their comrades shattering and disappearing, the remaining Demons tried to re-enter the anomaly to reach safety. The Fallen Angel seeing the mass defection rushed to beat them to it and standing between them and their means of escape he levelled both hands at his own creations spraying them with the deadly blue arcs of light emitted from his fingers. The first couple of Demons fell in disintegrating piles of flesh and slime. The Demons behind halted their rush forward and following a shouted instruction from the Angel turned back to Ilyas' team in a frenzied attack. Before they had gone five or six strides, all three Nephilim had opened fire. It was like shooting rats in a barrel. The frenzied creatures had no chance. Within seconds all were dead, dissolving before their eyes. Amy looked up to the Angel staring at the carnage. She steadied her weapon with both hands. The look on his face was pure hatred but before she could react and fire at him he had turned and disappeared through the anomaly which instantly closed behind him.

Mark let out a whoop of triumph. Amy turned bewildered eyes to Ilya. "Why didn't he fight?"

"I suspect he is reporting our presence to his commander as we speak. I suggest we get out of here as quickly as possible. Taking down Demons is easy. I wouldn't want to be here if a troop of Fallen Angels come back with vengeance on their minds."

Without delay they back-tracked to the Land Rover and then put a few miles between themselves and the site of the anomaly before Ilya reported back to Ralph with news of their success. Their euphoria quickly evaporated when Ralph informed them that anomalies were erupting at a phenomenal rate and he was unable to send any reinforcements to their location and they would have to continue alone. Ilya nodded grimly at this information. He had his cell phone on speaker so Mark and Amy were aware of the situation.

"So we carry on as we are." He said not meeting their eyes, "They know we're onto them now so we need to be extra vigilant. He replaced his phone into his jacket before turning to the rear of the vehicle to distribute more ammunition.

"Do you think they'll use the same anomaly?" Amy asked

"There's no knowing. We'll drive back that way but I'll park up further away just in case they have reappeared. We'll try to keep the element of surprise in our favour." He drove back towards Prawle Point in silence, both Amy and Mark locked in their own thoughts. It was now fully dark and it had started to rain. The isolated area had taken on an eerie atmosphere as Ilya pulled up in a 'passing place' on the narrow lane about a quarter of a mile from where they had previously parked. They quietly got out of the vehicle and stood silently listening for any tell-tale sounds from the lane leading down to the point jutting out into the English Channel. The rain had by now turned quite heavy and Amy pulled her collar up as it began to trickle down her neck. All three were wearing padded body protecting vests and she was acutely aware of the added weight. She had no idea if this type of body armour afforded any protection from whatever the Fallen Angels could use against them but it was known to resist the teeth and claws of Demons.

"Okay..." Ilya whispered, "be careful...don't forget your training. Keep in contact with your cell phones...and good luck." He added. "Meet back here in one hour...right."

Mark and Amy nodded before stealthily heading along the unlit lane. Not far from where the original anomaly had opened, the lane petered out into flat scrubland leading down to the sea. Ilya directed with his hand for them to spread out. Within seconds they were out of view of each other each treading carefully over the rough bracken strewn ground listening as they searched for their prey. The rain was now heavier and Amy constantly wiped her eyes with the back of her hand. Her mind wandered to thinking how many times her mother must have been involved in this sort of expedition and she felt comforted by the knowledge that she was following in her footsteps. She had no idea how long she had been furtively tracking through the darkness but she slowly became aware that she also didn't know how close the other team members were. She stopped and listened and hearing nothing she licked her dry lips before moving on. This is what she was trained for...she could do this. She had only gone three or four strides when suddenly from her left she heard something moving from beyond the treeline. She dropped to her knees cocking her pistol as she peered into the darkness. Was it one of the team? Should she call out to check? But if it wasn't one of her colleagues, she would be giving away her location. She waited, the damp from the ground soaking into her knees. She hastily wiped the rain from her eyes again whilst trying to hold her weapon steady. Suddenly, giving her no time to react, a Goblin rushed at her on its squat ungainly legs. A cry of astonishment escaped her as she braced for the impact of its attack. It was much shorter than her and as she was kneeling, it hit her square in the chest. Instinctively from her training she fell backwards, grabbing its arms and bucking her legs so that her feet caught the creature in the abdomen hurling it upwards and over her head to come crashing a few feet behind her. Recoiling from the revulsion of the jelly-like feel of its body she was back on her knees facing the sprawled body not five foot away from her. Her gun had been knocked from her hand and she unsuccessfully searched the bracken strewn ground for it. Within seconds the creature had found its footing and had turned to face her again. As she was feeling amongst the wet mud and leaf litter, her hand made contact with a broken branch...it would have to do. As the Goblin lunged at her again she thrust the makeshift weapon upwards into its throat. The yell it tried to emit came out as a watery gurgle before it exploded into fragments soaking her in ooze. Hastily she turned her face away but not before her cheeks had been liberally soaked. She turned away retching and shuddering from the horror of it. Eventually she stopped gagging and rested back on her haunches trying to calm her erratic rapid breathing. After a minute or two she became aware of the darkness around her and she listened for any other sounds to reveal if Ilya or Mark were anywhere near. She stood up, ears straining to make sense of a distant commotion. She could tell that the sounds were coming from some distance away but it was clear that something large was wildly hurtling through the darkness. Surely neither of her colleagues would make such a racket. Whatever was heading her way was not attempting to keep the noise down. Suddenly the terrifying realisation hit her that whatever it was, it was clearly crashing through the undergrowth in her direction and would be upon her within seconds. Turning, she fled back the way she had come, entering the sparse treeline hoping to remain undetected now that she had no weapon with which to defend herself. She had no idea which direction to take; she just stumbled onwards trying to put as much distance between herself and whatever it was. She ignored the brambles that caught at her clothes, catching in her hair and scratching her hands and face in her panic-stricken flight. She was only aware that something was close on her tail and gaining by the second. Before she could register it, she went crashing down a steep slippery bank tumbling over and over into a shallow stream. The wind had been knocked out of her and in vain she tried to clamber up the opposite bank to escape the freezing water that was rapidly soaking into her clothes. At this point she heard the victorious howl of a dreaded Demon and turning her head saw it atop the bank that she had slid down cackling at her vain attempts to scramble out of the water. So this was what terror felt like. She closed her eyes, covering her head with her hands and making herself as small as she could, she waited for the thing to leap on top of her. She heard the creature give a bellow and she tensed waiting for the attack. Seconds ticked by and although the Demon continued to howl, it did not leap down on top of her as she expected. She risked a glance from under one arm and was stupefied to see that the creature had turned and was bellowing at something behind it, appearing to have completely forgotten about her lying half submerged in the stream. She lowered one arm so that she could see more clearly what had caused the distraction. As she stared open mouthed, the Demon exploded and toppled towards her. Once again she braced herself for an impact but before that could happen, it had completely disappeared. What was going on? What had killed it as it had poised to attack her? Lowering both arms she strained to see through the darkness. Her ears now detected the sound of the wind…no not the wind but a sound akin to it. With a rush of flying feathers and the wild beating of wings an Angel materialised on the bank above her where moments before the Demon had stood cackling at her. It was too dark to see his face but there was enough moonlight to reveal that he was heavily armoured. He seemed not to see Amy half submerged in the water and cowering against the muddied bank. He hastily scanned the area where the Demon had been. Unable to stop herself Amy began to slide back down the bank causing the Angel to quickly look in her direction. Something in his stance caused the shock of recognition to tear through her and in an instant she comprehended that the recognition wasn't mutual for he lifted his right arm pointing straight at her chest. She didn't even have time to call out his name. As his fingers flexed to send a killing beam of powerful light at her, she called out to him using her mind...*MALCHEDIEL!*

In a fraction of a second he swung his arm away from her and at the same time clenched his fist. A flash of blue light sparked through his curled fingers streaking up his forearm before fading to nothingness. Amy's eyes never left his face as he stood above her staring back at her, shaking his arm out to the side to ease the pain that racked his limb from fingers to shoulder. He quickly removed his helmet throwing it to the ground before scrambling down the embankment towards her. His hair was matted to his head with sweat. There was blood trickling down his thigh from a flesh wound and he was streaked with mud. The rain was running down his face in rivulets but to her, he looked wonderful. She reached up to him with open arms, sobs escaping through trembling lips but he didn't touch her. He stood looking down at her, his legs astride her body. He let out an oath in his native tongue as he glared at her. She tried to scramble to her feet but toppled backwards into the water as the pain from a wrenched ankle seared through her. If she expected a loving pair of arms to enfold her she was to be disappointed. He remained standing breathing heavily scowling at her. "What in the saints names are you doing here!" he threw at her. Stung by his coldness she stared back at him unable to think of an answer to his angry retort. "I could have killed you." He went on, "are you insane?"

Realisation of this fact was sinking in and the tears flowed faster as she tried to push herself up by bracing her back against the bank behind. Her feet skidded in the mud as she endeavoured to stand before him. The weight of her soaking clothes added to the heavy body armour made the effort almost impossible and finally Malchediel reached down to help her to her feet. She stood braced on one leg unable to put any weight on her injured ankle. "Are you alone?" he asked shortly.

She sniffed before answering, "I was with two comrades but I don't know where they are now."

He stood scowling at her and she timidly added, "We got split up."

He made an impatient sound and she couldn't stop another tear from rolling down her cheek at the way he was treating her. What had happened to the loving Malchediel that she had known? She didn't recognise this cold angry person before her. He shook his head at her before stooping to sweep her up into his arms. His wings that had been held flat against his back pulsed two strong beats, carrying them both back up to the bank where he set her back down onto her one good leg before retrieving his helmet. Once he had replaced it on his head he swooped her back up into his arms and took off again through the relentless rain. Trying not to dwell on his strange behaviour she nestled in his arms drawing warmth from his body. It was not easy given that he was wearing a breastplate but his arms were strong and comforting. She had no idea where he was taking her. She assumed he was looking below for her friends so it was with some surprise when she saw that they were approaching a cliff face above the sea. The moon glinted off the surf below but she had no idea where they were. She was shivering from the cold as she watched him skirt the sandstone cliff face before hovering before a cave entrance some thirty or forty feet above the sea. He appeared to be sensing whether the cave may be a safe place to enter. Evidently he decided that it was, and he entered the cavernous opening lowering Amy carefully within the dark interior. The wind which had been blowing briskly without was unnoticeable inside the cave and Amy's chattering teeth could clearly be heard in the silence. Malchediel removed his helmet once more and dropped it to the ground. The metallic clatter reverberated around the cavern. Without looking at her he said curtly, "Get your clothes off."

"What?"

Now he looked at her, "Take you clothes off. You're freezing cold and they're soaking wet." Then he turned away removing his breastplate after unbuckling the straps at the side. She stood shivering staring at him for a few moments before doing as he asked. With trembling fingers she unzipped her body vest and let it fall to the ground relived to be free of its weight. She glanced back at him watching as he unbuckled his greaves and vambraces. He looked up. "Take them all off." He added. "I can't warm you if you keep those wet things on."

Oh my...he wants me naked. She thought, but she obeyed. Once she had removed all her wet clothing she looked back at him to see that he too was naked. If she hadn't been so cold and shivering so violently she thought she may have glowed at the sheer sight of him. He reached for her hand and pulled her to him, sitting down on the hard stone floor he eased her down onto his lap. She caught her breath as her body came into contact with his. He felt so warm and firm she almost forgot the pain in her ankle. He made no move to touch her sexually but he wrapped his arms around her holding her close to his body tucking her legs between his so that her feet rested on top of his. Then leaning forwards he bought his wings around so that they too enveloped her in a warm cocoon. Within minutes the heat from his body began to seep into her and the chattering teeth slowly stilled. He rested his chin against the top of her head and without another word relaxed against her. Within minutes he sensed that she was asleep.

Malchediel didn't need to sleep. He sat motionless holding Amy close, not wanting to admit to himself that her soft curvaceous body was having the effect of almost making him forget that she had turned her back on him when he had most needed her...almost, almost. Whilst she was asleep he could pretend that all was well between them and she still loved him.

Chapter Ten

Ilya and Mark between them only encountered three small pockets of Demons during the rest of that night. As dawn broke they contacted one another by cell phone and met up back at the Land Rover. Neither was able to locate Amy's whereabouts. Ilya reported back to Ralph that they had lost contact with her and was told to wait another hour for her to return to the vehicle. When she didn't, and they had been unable to reach her by phone they decided to split up and do a daytime search for her. It was at about nine o'clock that Mark found her cell phone half embedded in the muddied bank of a stream. A careful search of the area revealed considerable activity on both banks of the stream but no sign of Amy herself. They were puzzled at the complete disappearance of their comrade and continued to search the area without success. At this point both officers were beginning to think that she was lying dead somewhere or that she had been taken captive although that had never been known to happen before. By ten o'clock they contacted Ralph again who instructed them to return to the farmhouse from where a more detailed search could be planned using more people.

Neither Ilya nor Mark wanted to leave with Amy still missing but it made no sense to search the same area over and over. Later they would expand the search area with more officers. Within a couple of hours they were back at the farmhouse in Cornwall and after giving Ralph brief details of what had gone on at Prawle Point the exhausted duo were allowed to get a little sleep.

Meanwhile back within the cave above the crashing waves Amy slept on in Malchediel's arms. He pondered on how he had come upon Amy stranded and injured in the stream. He too had earlier detected a small group of Demons left unattended further upstream from where Amy had fallen. He had despatched them all with the exception of one, who had escaped charging through the undergrowth. Following it, he finally caught up with it on the bank of the stream. After quickly killing it, he became aware of something moving in the water. He shuddered when he remembered how close he had come to killing Amy thinking she was another Demon or Goblin.

He adjusted his position causing Amy to give a little moan of irritation at being disturbed and despite himself he smiled at her reaction. His hand still smarted from the withheld fireball that he had clenched in his fist. Thank the saints that he had picked up her telepathic frenzied shout. How would he have come to terms with being the cause of her death? He was angry with her over her betrayal but he still loved her...would that ever change?

Daylight had crept into the cave and eventually Amy stirred. Malchediel loosened his hold on her and allowed her time to wake properly. As she began to move against him, his body responded to the softness of her skin against his. He rested his lips against her hair but resisted the urge to actually press a kiss against her. Whilst she slept he had allowed himself the pleasure of gently stroking her back but she would not know about that. Now that she slowly stretched against him yawning he refrained from any form of caressing, just supporting her in his arms. Suddenly she became aware of where she was and sat upright on his lap. She remembered that they were both naked and as his wings slowly opened, unfolding from around her she felt a hot flush creep up her face. She remained still for a moment not knowing what to say to him. He saved her the embarrassment of being the first to break the silence.

"Well…at least you're warm now." He said and even to his own ears, it sounded curt.

"Um…yes…thank you." She was acutely aware of his eyes upon her. She knew that she needed a shower. She had been almost completely submerged in a dirty muddy stream. Her hair must look bedraggled and she wished more than anything that she could brush her teeth. She glanced quickly up at his face and she melted from within at how beautiful he looked. His blue eyes bright and clear, his golden blonde hair now dry, falling softly over his shoulders. No-one she thought should look this good after spending a night sitting upright in a cave. She smiled tentatively at him but was disappointed not to get a response from him.

"Do you think you can stand?" he asked pointedly. In answer, she wriggled forward along his thighs, her face colouring again at the jolt of pleasure the feeling gave her. Favouring her good leg she stood unsteadily but found that trying to put any weight on her sprained ankle caused her to catch her breath. Malchediel was on his feet in a second steadying her with a hand under her elbow. They stood for a moment or two awkwardly looking at one another and she thought how ridiculous the situation must appear, both of them naked in a cave barely touching one another. Releasing her so that she stood on one leg, the other held at an angle free of any weight, he went to where she had left her clothes the night before. They were still a little damp and she watched in amazement as he laid them out and then hit them with a prolonged burst of light from his fingertips. Her mouth dropped open as she witnessed the rising steam as each item dried before her eyes. Within a few minutes he handed them to her avoiding her glance as she took them from him. As she scrambled into them he used the same technique to dry his own clothes and by the time she was dressed he had started to dress himself. She watched hoping that he would just glance and smile her way but he never did.

believe you were allowed to go off hunting on your own like that."

She felt like a child being chastised. "We had been working as a team. There were three of us. I guess I must have wandered further than I thought." She kept her eyes averted from his as she added, "I don't know how far I ran after I lost my pistol. I just wanted to put as much space between me and that thing."

"Hmmphh...I doubt you would ever out-run a Demon Amy." He emphasised the point with a slight shake of his head, "By the saints do you realise how close you came to being killed." He saw that his words had had a sobering effect on her. Her lip trembled leaving him feeling guilty. He grinned and winked at her, "Good thing I turned up when I did eh?"

After getting a tentative smile from her he stood up, "If you've had enough I think we had better try to find your comrades." He picked up his helmet and fastened it to one of the straps of his breastplate so that it hung down against his left hip. "I didn't see any sign of Demons or any of the Fallen whilst I was out. Perhaps the rest of your team eliminated that little pocket of evil. Where were you supposed to eventually meet up with the others?"

Armed with the information that their vehicle had been left at the end of the tarmac road near to Prawle Point, Malchediel with Amy in his arms headed that way scanning the ground below. There was a temporary respite to the unremitting rain of the past few days and it didn't take them long to get to where Amy had last seen her comrades. However on reaching the point where the road petered out into scrubland the Land Rover was missing. "They must have gone back to the Farmhouse." Amy said. She saw Malchediel scowl. He was angry that they had left her to her fate. *Oh hell...He's going to let fly when we finally meet up with the others.* She wasn't looking forward to it. She gave him directions of where to go next and as he took to the air once more she rested her head against his breastplate. As her arms went around his neck she hoped that his ill temper would ease before they reached Ralph's temporary base.

Chapter Eleven

Their approach to the Farm was witnessed by a number of the team who had been standing clustered around the vehicles parked haphazardly in the yard. As Malchediel landed with his customary ease several pairs of eyes were turned their way in astonishment. Amy heard his sharp intake of breath.

"Mal," she warned, "Please be nice."

Without looking at her he murmured, "I'm always nice."

"Please…" she added, "No scenes."

He exhaled through his nose.

Oh dear…he's not happy.

Suddenly, Ruby broke from the group with a squeal of delight. "Amy! Oh Amy…" She rushed forward as Malchediel's grip tightened on Amy still held in his arms.

"She has injured her ankle." He said shortly, "Please be careful." He eased her down into a standing position still supporting her around her waist. Not to be put off Ruby threw her arms around her friend hugging her, babbling incoherently how she had feared never to see her again. Ralph was the next to stride over to them. "You must be Malchediel." He said holding out his hand as though he were meeting the friend of a team member. "Amy has described you to us."

Malchediel made no attempt to shake the proffered hand staring coolly at the Team Leader. "And you are?" he said.

Amy cringed. *Oh…he's going to make the most of this.* She nudged him with her hip in warning. He didn't acknowledge the hint in any way.

"I'm the N.F.F. Team Leader down here, Ralph Roberts." Amy was pleased to see that he wasn't going to be cowed by a Warrior Angel. *Good for him.* He continued to extend his hand giving Malchediel no option other than having to shake it, although briefly.

"Do your team members make a habit of abandoning one of their own?" he asked coldly.

Without any show of embarrassment which impressed Amy no end Ralph answered, "Not at all, in fact Ilya and Mark searched for hours looking for Amy finding only her weapon and phone. They returned less than an hour ago for reinforcements to mount another search." He held the Angels' gaze without flinching, "We were just about to leave to head back to where she was last seen." Without waiting for an answer he turned to Amy, "I'm so relieved you're okay Amy."

"She has a sprained ankle." Malchediel repeated, "So not okay. I found her half drowned in a river fighting off a Demon...alone."

"Oh...Mal, it wasn't as bad as you make it sound." Amy put in, "It was more of a stream and I lost my footing." She nudged him more forcibly this time, trying to make light of it. I don't think I was in any danger of drowning."

"And the Demon?" Malchediel asked pointedly, "He just wanted to get to know you I suppose?"

Ruby giggled her arm still around Amy's shoulder.

"Yes...well...alright...I was glad you came along." Amy conceded.

As if on cue it began to rain diffusing the situation.

"Well, as we don't need to mount a search party any longer...shall we all get inside." Ralph smiled warmly refusing to be baited by an irate Angel.

Amy was well impressed with his composure.

Flexing his shoulders Malchediel retracted his wings to the delight of Ruby who had never seen an Angel before let alone spoken to one. Sweeping Amy back into his arms Malchediel followed the others into the Farmhouse.

"Okay, you've had your fun, now stop it." Amy hissed in his ear so no one else could hear. "These are my friends." She was relieved to see his lips twitch in amusement. "You're a wicked Angel." She whispered into his breastplate, not looking at him but feeling the supressed chuckle rise in his chest.

An hour later everyone was aware of what had occurred over the past twenty four hours. Amy concluded that there was nothing Ilya and Mark could have done differently following her and Malchediel leaving the area to seek shelter from the torrential rain. Ralph who had basic medical knowledge thanks to regular courses with the St John's Ambulance organisation had strapped up Amy's ankle and after taking pain killing tablets she felt more comfortable. She was aware of the fascination Malchediel's appearance was conjuring amongst the team. Ralph, thanks to his diplomacy had thawed Mal's earlier hostility and was now engaged in deep conversation. He was learning much about the attacks mounted by the Fallen using water as a medium with which to break through from the infernal to the corporeal realm inhabited by humans. "Why is this happening now?" Ralph asked. "After millennia of relative stability, why are we under attack to such a degree?"

"My guess is that Lucifer feels he has endured banishment long enough. The Creator consistently refuses forgiveness thus allowing the Fallen the chance to return. They have little to lose. If they cannot regain what they have lost they will destroy what God treasures the most...his great experiment...the human race."

"But surely God has the power to stop all of this. He is Almighty after all."

Malchediel gave a short laugh but there was little humour detectable. "He will not be held to ransom in this way. If He were to pit His might against the Fallen He would be giving credence to their ability to draw Him into a battle to decide who is the most powerful."

A look of shocked comprehension crossed Ralph's face.

"Exactly!" Malchediel confirmed. "If we, the faithful cannot defeat Lucifer and his followers then humankind stands alone."

"That is one sobering comment. Are we talking Armageddon here?"

Malchediel met Ralph's eyes with a steady gaze. "I think it would be prudent to pray that either they decide not to proceed with this madness or that if they do, they are not the victors." Leaving Ralph to digest his comment he stood and walked over to where Amy was quietly talking to Ruby.

"I need to check on things out there." He said with a nod to the door leading outside. Amy nodded, as Ruby looked up at Malchediel with rapture clearly etched on her face. In all the time that the two girls had been talking, Amy noted with amusement how her friend kept looking over at the Angel unable to stop herself displaying open admiration. As Mal strapped on his breastplate she commented, "Amy said that you normally work as part of a team…There are four of you I think she said."

Amy smiled inwardly as he turned what could only be described as a heart-stopping smile on Ruby.

"I do. I made a small detour to this area when I detected Demon presence. I will eventually have to join with my comrades but I would like to leave this area free of any threat before I go." He had lifted a foot onto a chair so that he could buckle on one of his greaves and missed the look of anguish that crossed Amy's face. She had only just become re-acquainted with the love of her life and he was talking of leaving her again. Within minutes he was back in full armour. He looked down into her face. "I shall be back before dark. Keep your weight off that foot." He added as he turned for the door.

"Oh my God Amy," Ruby drawled looking towards the door as it closed upon Malchediel, "How I envy you. That is one fit specimen."

Despite her feeling of despondency Amy spluttered a laugh at her friend's description of him. "I've heard of some classic adjectives to describe an Angel but 'fit' is a new one on me."

Ruby grinned, "I take your point but you have to admit there isn't much in the way of Angelic countenance but a hell of a lot of sexual chemistry going on there." She pursed her lips, "He positively smoulders when he looks at you…"

Amy was about to protest but Ruby went on, "Aw, come on there's more than saving your soul on his mind…like I said I'm envious."

Amy quickly looked around the room to check if they could be overheard. "Ruby!" she hissed, "This is an Angel we're talking about. He's not supposed to form relationships with the likes of us." She glanced over to where Ralph and Ilya were talking before adding quietly, "You know what it could mean for him."

Ruby quirked an eyebrow, "Yes I do but if you ask me he's gone beyond the bounds of caution. I don't think anything has changed for him since the night he was abducted. Giving her friend a knowing look she added, "I think you probably harbour the same feelings too."

Amy looked away. How could she answer that? She knew it was true.

Both girls turned to Ralph as he called across the room. "He is coming back I assume?"

Amy was glad of the change of subject. Ruby's observation on the possible relationship between her and Malchediel was becoming uncomfortable. "Yes. He's just making an assessment of the area. He said he would be back before dark."

"Hmm…" Ralph glanced at the screen in front of him, "There's no activity showing at the moment. Hopefully he'll be able to confirm if they intend to show themselves again or if they have abandoned the area for a different location."

"They have us over a barrel don't they?" chipped in Ilya, "They can materialise anywhere near water. We are just marking time rushing from one area to another trying to eliminate them as they appear."

Ralph did not answer but his grim expression spoke volumes.

Malchediel returned to the Farmhouse as it was beginning to get dark. "The armour was unnecessary." He said as he began to unfasten his breastplate. "There was no sign of Demon activity nor could I detect any anomalies." He sat down bending to undo the greaves before placing them with the body armour on the table. Amy watched his fluid movements as he finally laid the vambraces alongside his other armour with a clatter of metal on metal. She knew that technically Angels did not sleep but she thought how tired he looked anyway with dark shadows beneath his eyes. The effect was to give him a more ethereal appearance and her heart melted knowing that he had been working day and night for weeks trying to keep on top of what was happening. Trying to protect a species that had no idea he and his like even existed.

"Do you think they have abandoned this area then?" Ralph asked.

"It would seem so. I believe they are trying to find a location where they will not be disturbed so that they can bring forth multitudes of their Demons readying them for a mass attack. Fortunately they need water to produce an anomaly. Unfortunately the planet is covered in suitable areas in which to manifest them." He looked towards Ralph, "Clearly living on an island like Britannia is not the best place to be right now."

Ralph nodded, then giving a sigh he stood making his way to the kitchen. "I suggest we eat and get an early night. We may as well make our way back to base tomorrow as soon as it gets light. The Doctor may want to send us to another location from there."

As the two girls were sharing a room at the farmhouse, Amy was unable to speak privately with Malchediel until the next morning. After breakfast everyone busied themselves packing all their equipment into the vehicles in the farmyard. Amy, because she could not put much weight on her injured ankle waited inside with Malchediel. There was so much she wanted to say to him but now that they were briefly alone she found that she did not know how to convey her feelings to him. "Mal…" she began tentatively but before she could go on he broke in.

"Nothing has changed for me Amy. I still want to be with you."

Tears came unbidden to her eyes at his declaration. "Ohh Mal…I thought you hated me." She gulped on a sob, "I knew that I shouldn't have returned the feather the way I did… and when you didn't come back to me I realised that I had ruined everything." She dashed away the tears on her cheeks as he swiftly came to where she was sitting with one leg propped up on a chair. He knelt before her looking up into her face. "I understand now why you did that. You would have had no other option than to comply with Nemamiah's mind play. I will be taking that up with him when I next see him." He added a smile lifting the corners of his mouth. He stroked her cheeks with the pads of his thumbs wiping the tears away before kissing her gently. She held her breath as his lips lingered against hers. "I love you." He whispered and she felt his words against her mouth igniting a passion deep within her. Her hands came up behind his head holding him in place against her parted lips. Lifting his hair so that she could stroke his neck she murmured "I never thought I would hear you say those words ever again my love."

At that moment the door to the farmyard opened without warning and Ruby strode through. "Okay, that's everyth…." She stopped short taking in the sight of Malchediel on his knees with Amy's arms around his neck. "Oops…sorry…" she uttered turning on her heel and going back outside pulling the door to, behind her. At her intrusion Malchediel and Amy sprang apart but too late they had been observed. They stared at one another before Amy burst into giggles just as there was a loud knock at the door. Malchediel smiled before calling out, "You can come in Ruby."

Ruby's grinning face appeared around the door, "Sorry about that." She said before coming back into the room as Malchediel stood up moving a step away from Amy.

"I just came to say that we're almost ready to leave. Ralph has asked me to check all the rooms to make sure we haven't left anything behind." Turning to Malchediel she asked, "Are you coming back with us?"

"No…" he said hesitantly looking down at Amy for her reaction, "I need to get back to my comrades. They know where I am and they know that there have been problems here. I will need to inform them of what has gone on over the past few days."

"I see…okay I had better do a quick check before we lock the place up then."

Whilst Ruby ran upstairs to make sure that nothing had been left in any of the bedrooms Amy took the opportunity to ask, "When will I see you again?"

"I will come to your base as soon as I can get away. By the way, your little Nephilim friend is still as prickly as he ever was."

Amy frowned before realising that he was referring to Stephen. "Stephen? You've seen Stephen?"

"Oh yes, I went looking for you and when I found that you had sold the shop I confronted him. I had no idea where you had gone. I couldn't check with Raguel who would have known your whereabouts because to all intents and purposes you were a part of my past. Stephen was my only hope of finding you."

"Oh I see…what do you mean 'he was as prickly as ever?'"

Malchediel rolled his eyes, "Well…he was never my number one fan was he? But he seemed to think that I had abandoned you. He took pleasure in using some obscenity to describe me."

"Oh no, what did he say?"

"It doesn't matter. I would probably have had the same reaction under the circumstances."

At this point Ruby came skipping back downstairs with a sweater, "Good thing I checked. Mark left this in his room. If you help Amy into one of the vehicles, I'll check downstairs and then I can lock up."

Malchediel collected his armour and deposited them on the porch outside before coming back to lift Amy into his arms to carry her outside. "I can probably walk with a little assistance Mal." She said as he swung her up holding her close.

"You probably can but this is more for my benefit than yours. I like to carry you."

She did not protest further because she liked to be carried by him as well.

The team were standing talking amongst themselves as Malchediel carried Amy across the farmyard to one of the waiting vehicles. Most of them turned to watch as he carefully placed her onto the back seat of the black BMW. "This is going to cause some comments back at the Hall you know." Amy said as Malchediel reached over to fasten her safety belt. He looked up at her face as he bent over her noticing that she was blushing from all the attention they were getting. He grinned mischievously, "Shall I kiss you goodbye, just to add a little spice for them?"

"Don't you dare!" she hissed in his ear.

His smile broadened as their eyes met. He lingered not moving away from her, and as his smile slowly faded he spoke quietly, "They'll know soon enough what is going on between us Amy. I don't intend to lose you again." He adjusted his position so that he was squatting outside the car looking up into her face. "I have to go back now but I will be coming back to you just as soon as I can."

Amy caught a movement out of the corner of her eye. "They're coming over Mal." Then quickly added, "Are you sure this is what you want?"

whispered with a smile as she lay back against the pillows pulling him down with her.

He was experienced in so many ways that excited and aroused feelings in her that she never knew she possessed, but why should that surprise her. He had lived for millennia and she, but for two decades. Of course he would be an experienced lover. She eagerly returned his kisses catching her breath as he slowly unbuttoned the pyjama jacket that she was wearing. She watched his face as his eyes travelled over her. He bent back towards her, lightly kissing her throat, planting light kisses down her sternum. She moaned softly when he pulled back a little, to rest the tip of his tongue against her breastbone trailing it slowly, enticingly down to her navel. She murmured his name as she gave herself over to him completely and utterly.

She became aware of the dawn chorus beyond the window. The birds that had roosted in silence overnight beginning to welcome a new day. She stretched luxuriously but then caught her breath sharply as Malchediel rested his hand on her abdomen generating a pulse of heat to pass through her. It passed quickly and she wondered if she had imagined it. "What was that?" she asked.

"Just making sure that there are no implications from what we have done." He said matter-of-factly.

She frowned at his words not comprehending their meaning but within a few seconds realisation dawned on her. "You mean...that was some form of birth control?"

"Any unplanned issue would complicate matters Amy." Was all he said by way of explanation.

Chapter Twelve

The enormity of what they had done only occurred to Amy later as she lay cocooned in Malchediel's protective arms. She had woken early and found that she was unable to go back to sleep. For some time she lay immersed in post coital bliss, her head resting in the crook of his arm, her right hand against his chest. She revelled in the steady rise and fall and the even beat of his heart. Then as the euphoria of his love making melted away a feeling of dread slowly took its place.

"Mal…" she whispered.

"Hmmm?" His fingers stroked along her upper arm.

"What we've done…does that mean you can never go back?"

There was a moments' pause before he answered and those few seconds confirmed what she feared. He turned his head, resting his lips against her head. Very gently he kissed her hair. "I regret nothing Amy." He spoke quietly, his lips still against her head. "I love you. I couldn't imagine my life if it wasn't with you."

She moved back against the crook of his elbow so that she could see his face. "But to never return to the only life you have ever known my love…I'm scared that one day you will regret what you have done. I couldn't bear it if one day you find that you blame me, maybe even grow to hate me." Her voice trailed away.

He moved his arm easing away from her so that they were face to face. "Amy…the world is about to change. Who knows what the future will bring. All we know for certain is that mankind faces the biggest threat of all time albeit they know nothing of what is going to transpire. All I know is that whatever happens we will be together. He bent towards her and kissed her gently at first but as she began to respond, stroking his back, he groaned raising himself so that he was hunched over her, resting his weight on his forearms either side of her.

"You know what that does to me." He murmured huskily.

She grinned up at him but before she could reply they both turned towards the door where the knob was rattling sharply.

"Amy! Amy it's me. The door is locked. Are you awake?" It was Ruby.

The lovers looked at one another before both erupting into fits of giggles.

"Hold on Ruby, I'm coming." Amy wriggled from under Malchediel's arms and sat up reaching for the pyjama jacket that had been hastily discarded earlier. As she buttoned it up, she regarded Malchediel now sitting upright, his golden hair tousled and hanging over his shoulders. His blue eyes glittering with amusement as her cheeks began to colour. "Let me do the talking." She said nervously.

He shrugged his shoulders clearly looking forward to how she would explain having a naked Angel in her bed. At the door she turned back to where he sat up in her bed, the sheets rumpled around his waist. It wouldn't take a genius to work out that he was naked and his 'mussed' hair clearly indicated some form of recent vigorous activity. He clearly was feeling none of the embarrassment at being caught in flagrante that now racked Amy as she viewed her lover before turning back to open the door.

Ruby practically fell into the room as the door opened. "You don't normally lock the door. What were..." She stopped in mid-sentence as her eyes alighted on Malchediel grinning rakishly from the bed. "Good Morning Ruby. How pleasant to see you again." He barely heard Amy's groan of mortification from where she stood, hand still resting on the door knob. Ruby looked quickly at Amy and then back to Malchediel who was casually sitting with just a bed-sheet over him, an arm draped across one raised knee.

"Um…um… What are you doing here?" she asked in a fluster.

Before he had a chance to answer, Amy caught hold of Ruby's arm and propelling her back onto the landing closed the door of her room behind them but not before they both heard Malchediel's amused laughter.

"Can we speak in your room?" she asked still guiding Ruby back along the corridor to the next bedroom. By the time they reached her door, Ruby had regained her equilibrium. "I'd rather have stayed in your room. That's some eye candy you have in your bed." She sniggered.

Whilst Amy was being grilled by Ruby over Malchediel's nocturnal arrival at St Alexandra Hall, Malchediel himself tried to make telepathic contact with Nemamiah. For the first time in all the millennia that they had been friends all he encountered was a black void. The realisation that he was now excluded from his old life shocked him. He hadn't expected his fall to be implemented so quickly. His dismay was tinged with anger. He had fallen in love with a mortal…not such a crime surely? He didn't consider himself a Fallen Angel. He would never harm humans. He still thought of himself as a Warrior committed to protecting mankind but because he had broken the rules he was now shut out. He had to get used to standing alone. He would work alongside the Nephilim from now on, but the thought of having to contend with their limited powers did little to instil confidence in him.

By the time Amy returned with Ruby in tow, he had dressed in what little clothing he possessed. Amy regarded him across the room in his customary cropped trousers. He was bare-chested which had allowed him to use his wings earlier. "We need to get you some clothes before you see Doctor Steenbergen." She said matter-of-factly.

She barely heard Ruby's murmured comment, "I like him as he is." before quickly elbowing her friend in the ribs. Ruby grimaced at the assault adding, "I'll go and get something suitable from Ralph. They're about the same size." And with that she left Amy and Malchediel alone.

"Well?" Malchediel ventured as the door closed behind Ruby.

"She came to tell me that we're on the move again. The Doctor is sending a team to Cheddar Reservoir. The control room has picked up heightened Demon activity there…God! They're popping up all over the place." She was rummaging in her wardrobe for clothes and didn't see Malchediel's frown at her blasphemous expletive. Stepping away holding a pair of combat trousers in her hand she went on, "you will come with us won't you?"

"Of course… Someone has to keep you safe."

She turned to glare at him but was mollified when he smiled back at her.

She had showered and was dressing back in the bedroom when Ruby returned with a pair of jeans and a sweater for Malchediel. "There's a briefing in the Doctor's office in fifteen minutes." She said handing the clothes over. I've told him that you're here." She added openly admiring the Angel's torso as he pulled the sweater over his head. He hooked his thumbs into the waistband of his trousers as if about to remove them but then glanced over to Ruby who was still standing watching him. "Okay Ruby we will see you there as soon as we're dressed," and waited for her response.

"Err…oh right…I'll see you there then." With a disappointed look on her face she left them to finish dressing. Malchediel chuckled once the door had closed. As he changed into the borrowed jeans Amy shook her head at him, "You tease her and then frustrate her…that's unkind." She said shaking her head at him. His smile broadened at her rebuke.

Amy was about to fasten the clasp on her watch when there was a knock at the door. "Come in Ruby." She called glancing at Malchediel.

The door opened and Doctor Steenbergen's head appeared, "Not Ruby...May I come in Amy?"

"Of course." She was flustered by his sudden appearance and very conscious of Malchediel standing close. "You are aware I think that Malchediel arrived early this morning?"

"Yes, yes Ruby told me." He nodded a greeting towards the Angel. "I just wanted a quick word with you both before the meeting." His demeanour gave nothing away and Amy wondered if he had any idea of what had gone on between them in that very room an hour or so ago. His next words confirmed that he had his suspicions.

"May I ask a very blunt question?" and without waiting for consent, he went on, "I have reason to believe that you have joined the realms of the Fallen."

The room was deathly quiet and Amy looked to Malchediel who stood looking stonily towards the Doctor.

"No." Mal answered coldly, "I have not joined with my Fallen brethren. I would not be standing here now if that were the case. I have been banished it is true for the sin of falling in love with a mortal. There is a difference. My loyalty to your cause has not altered. I will fight for your continued existence. I will just have to do it without my fellow Angels."

The two men stood eyes locked upon one another with Amy watching them both.

Finally the Doctor smiled, "That is what I was hoping to hear." He held his hand out and Malchediel shook it clearly relieved that the awkwardness had been overcome.

Amy let out the breath she had been holding as the Doctor turned towards the door, "Shall we get this briefing over with?"

Malchediel's first skirmish working alongside Nephilim fighters guaranteed his acceptance by them. They cleared the area around the Cheddar reservoir easily, closing down the anomaly before returning to the Hall with no casualties.

If he missed his former life he gave no indication of it. His presence at St Alexandra's was accepted by all and no comment was made regarding his relationship with Amy. They were accepted as a couple and the only awkwardness occurred when Stephen came for a weekend visit a few weeks after Malchediel had arrived. The two of them would never be friends but they grudgingly tolerated one another during their time together. Stephen returned to Cornwall following his two day tryst with Ruby.

There were regular exercises when teams went out to crush manifestations across the south west but with Malchediel's presence they were easily overcome.

It was on one of these 'call-outs' however that disaster struck.

A team of ten Nephilim including Amy, Ruby and Ralph accompanied Mal to a stretch of marshland near the coast where a dozen or so Demons had manifested. As usual all the team were wearing Nephilim body armour including Malchediel. He had abandoned his own armour when he had deserted his Celestial home. He didn't like or trust the padded jackets of the Nephilim but it was better than nothing.

In a short time they had eliminated most of the Demons but there was one huge ugly brute that fought like something demented and seemed immune to the Nephilim weapons. Mal and Amy were fighting side by side and he called over to her, "Use your telepathic powers...What is he afraid of?" Amy stepped back and focused her mind on the creature as he lashed out again and again at her fellow fighters. Holding his features in her mind she delved deep into his subconscious. Within seconds she saw his creator, a Fallen Angel. Golden haired much like Malchediel, his beautiful features cold and chiselled, a look of fury on his face. The Demon was terrified of his creator. He was fighting the Nephilim out of fear of the Angel that had called him forth. He was terrified of failure. If he failed, the Angel would destroy him. Even as Amy's mind saw the Demon's predicament, an anomaly opened up behind him and the very Angel appeared to goad his Demon to fight on. Mal took his chance and threw a bolt of light at its chest. It screamed out in pain but wasn't mortally wounded. It went down on one knee turning to the Fallen Angel for help. Its plea was in vain. The Angel sneered angrily at the beast as he sent a bolt of his own at the hapless creature before turning back and striding through the anomaly before it closed on itself. As normally happened, the Demon exploded as it died. Amy turned a look of triumph at Malchediel who returned a shout of jubilation back at her. Neither of them expected what happened next. As the creature disintegrated, one of its spines exploded from its tail flying towards Amy. She was punching the air in triumph exposing a small portion of her neck above her padded vest. She didn't see the spine hurtling towards her and only felt the sharp prickle as it hit and embedded itself in her neck. Malchediel's eyes widened in horror as she raised her hand to the small wound thinking it was a stinging insect. "Nooooooo!" he cried out as he stumbled towards her. Too late, her hand encountered the spine, no bigger than a child's crayon. She gripped it and pulled it free looking down to see what it was. She turned to Malchediel, a look of bemusement on her face. She could not understand why he was looking at her with such a look of dread. Then the pain hit her. Her neck felt as if it was on fire. Her eyes widened in fear as Mal caught her. She screamed, her hand clutched to her throat as her legs gave way. The scream went on and on as Malchediel eased her down so that she was cradled against his knee. She was gasping for breath, the scream dying to a gurgle, her eyes wide and pleading to her lover. "P..p..please..." she gasped, "Make it s...st..stop... Ahhhh..." she cried out in agony. The burning sensation travelling down her body. She was on fire. Drawing her knees up to her chest she retched again and again as the pain became unbearable. The searing burning heat went on and on until she thought she was going to die. Then her body went into spasm, her eyes rolled to the back of her head and she slipped into unconsciousness.

"AMY!" he cried holding her against him. Then turning his face skyward he screamed, "RAPHAEL...RAPHAEL. I NEED YOU! RAPH-AE-LLL." He was unaware of a growing crowd of Nephilim surrounding him. None had seen what had happened and were only now mindful of something terrible going on. Malchediel glanced quickly around him observing that there were no Demons left. Tears were streaming down his face and sobs were racking his body as he held Amy's unconscious form in his arms. Again he turned his face to the heavens screaming the one name, "RAPHAEL. PLEASE...RAPHAEL PLEASE... COME."

There was a rush of air and several of the Nephilim staggered back as a vicious wind stirred up leaves and debris. The air in front of Malchediel shimmered and pulsed as the shape of the Healer Archangel formed before him. "Malchediel." His voice was deep and resonant. "You have no right to call upon me. You are no longer one of us..."

"Please, please Raphael I did not call you here for me. Please help her..." He indicated the girl in his arms. She was pale but the wound on her neck had taken on a livid purple colour and was spreading down beneath her collar. "Please I'm begging you..."

"I can do nothing Malchediel. She is a mortal. I cannot treat her. You know that."

"Raphael, I have never begged in my life but I am now, please, please you cannot let her die."

The Archangel sighed, "This is not my choice. I can only heal Angels. She will die. I cannot interfere. You know it is forbidden."

Malchediel's cheeks were wet with tears, his words coming in choked sobs. "I cannot accept that you will let her die when you have the power to save her."

"There are reasons for these rules Malchediel." The Healer looked sadly at him. "Only Michael has the power to override such a decision."

"Then ask him. Ask him for permission. I will do anything you ask... just save her."

Raphael sighed again but closed his eyes and called upon the greatest of Archangels for assistance.

Everyone held their breath as the Healer stood in silent communication with a higher authority.

After what seemed several minutes but was little more than seconds, Raphael opened his eyes and looked down at Malchediel. A slow smile spread over his features. "It seems that you are favoured this day Malchediel." He went down on one knee and placed two fingers against the wound on Amy's neck. His lips moved in silent prayer before removing his hand and standing up. Without another word he looked upwards and several of the Nephilim gasped as the air around him again shimmered and paled as he slowly disappeared from sight.

A soft cry of relief escaped Malchediel as he gathered Amy to him and stood up holding her against his chest. Ralph pushed his way through the stunned Nephilim to where Malchediel stood cradling the form of Amy's limp body. "Bring her over to my vehicle," he said, "I'll drive her back to The Hall."

Malchediel shook his head. "It will be quicker if I take her." He said. "Will you hold her while I take off this cursed jacket?" He carefully handed the unconscious girl to Ralph before ripping off the body armour. Taking Amy back, he unfurled his wings and bracing his feet against the ground he pushed off, his wings beating strongly as he headed back towards Bath with the insensible Amy.

By the time the team of Nephilim reached the Hall by more conventional means Amy was in bed with Malchediel and the Doctor watching over her still unconscious form. The Doctor had checked all her vitals and pronounced that everything seemed normal considering that she had suffered a considerable trauma. Neither was inclined to leave her bedside until she regained consciousness. Whilst waiting for the team to return they talked together in hushed tones. Malchediel explained what had happened. "I knew that the worst thing she could do was to pull the spine out. They are barbed and as long as they are left alone there is no risk. They have to be cut out without damaging the barb. If pulled, they break off in the skin releasing toxins which to mortals is fatal. I called to her but she didn't hear me. As soon as she pulled it out I knew time was short." He caught his breath on a sob as he relived the scene at the coast.

The Doctor leaned forwards giving Mal's shoulder a reassuring squeeze. He drew in a breath, "I cannot understand how Raphael was given the go-ahead to heal Amy. As I understand it he only treats Angels. Why would the Archangel Michael give him permission to help a Nephilim girl?" He shook his head bemused. The same thought had occurred to Malchediel and he had no answer for it.

It was two days before Amy regained consciousness. Mal never left her bedside sitting silently holding one of her hands. Ruby visited her bedroom checking up on her condition regularly. It was late in the afternoon when Mal noticed her eyelids flickering as he gently traced circular movements across the back of her hand with his thumb. The movement stilled as he watched her face. After a few seconds her eyes opened and she looked up at the ceiling. "Amy…" he whispered. Slowly she turned her head towards him watching as his eyes pooled with tears, "Ohh Amy." He said again.

Her lips were cracked and dry as she tried to speak. He watched as her lips mouthed his name…"Malchediel."

Letting go of her hand he poured some water into a glass on the cupboard beside her bed. "Just a little sip." He said holding the glass to her lips. He supported her head gently as she greedily gulped down the liquid. "Steady…steady sweetheart." He urged, tilting the glass back so that she didn't choke. Her hand came up to cover his, her eyes never leaving his face. He eased her back down against the pillows, and herself from whatever was out there. "The Doctor is checking with other bases to see if they have come under attack as well."

"Hmm…Mal is with him now." Amy's voice was muffled as she slipped her padded vest over her head before fastening the side tabs. Bending down she retrieved her greaves and vambraces from the bottom of her locker before turning back to Ruby. "Who raised the alarm? Do you know?"

"Ilya was covering the control room overnight…I suppose he detected something."

Just at that moment Ilyas' head appeared around the doorway, "Are you ready girls?"

"Ilya…What's going on?" Ruby called.

I detected an anomaly near the lake about half an hour ago. By the time I roused the Doctor they were pouring through."

"Upstairs you said there were Angels as well. Did you mean Fallen Angels?" Amy questioned.

"There was Angelic presence showing on my screen and they were coming through the anomaly so I think it's safe to say they're from the opposition…Come on girls if you're ready the Doctor wants us in his office." And with that he turned on his heel and strode away across the hallway.

The great front door to the Hall was wide open spilling the Foyer lights out onto the driveway. It was barely light outside. Amy could see the sky streaked crimson, purple and gold. Cars were pulling up on the drive as Nephilim officers hurried into the building. Many had been called from their beds by the Doctor and Ilya to support those residing at the Hall.

"Listen everyone…Can I have your attention." The Doctor called standing in the doorway to his office. "About half an hour ago Ilya detected the opening of an anomaly at lakeside. There is quite a force there at the moment. They haven't attempted to move towards the Hall yet. They appear to be waiting to see what we are going to do. I have been in touch with London and Liverpool but they have detected nothing out of the ordinary. It looks as though this is an isolated incident. We have officers arriving as we speak as back-up. It could be that we have been chosen to test our strength when threatened. I have no idea how they managed to breach our defences. As you know we should be undetectable to the Fallen. This is something completely new to us." He glanced quickly at Malchediel standing at his shoulder. "We are fortunate in having Malchediel with us...I for one am grateful for that." A murmur ran through the assembled officers but then the Doctor went on, "Please be careful, all of you. God bless you and keep you safe."

Malchediel caught Amy's hand as the throng of Nephilim made their way to the double front doors.

"Remember...stay close to me." He whispered bending close to her ear.

As the dozen or so officers approached the ornamental lake they could see the hunched forms of at least sixty Demons. They seemed to be squatting on their haunches backs to the lake just staring out across the grounds towards the Hall. Behind them stood about six Fallen Angels standing almost casually looking over the heads of their creations at the approaching Nephilim. All had their wings unfurled and as the adrenalin coursed through her, Amy couldn't help but be overwhelmed at the beauty of them. It was now light enough for her to see their features clearly. All were as tall as Malchediel with perfectly proportioned bodies, broad shouldered and muscular. Two were blonde, the rest had dark hair. All wore it long to their shoulders. Suddenly one of them called out, "Malchediel...you appear to be on the wrong side." His companions laughed at the comment as he continued, "You're one of us now. Why fight on the losing side?" Whether the Demons could understand the Angel's words Amy had no idea but a few of them cackled most unpleasantly joining in with the laughter.

"I will never be one of you." Malchediel called back, "And what makes you think you could possibly be the winners in all of this?"

The spokesman for the Fallen sneered and answered, "Just look around you...What a motley crew you have allied yourself with." Again there was derisive laughter from his companions followed by the ugly cackling.

"I seem to recall that Asmodeus felt himself superior to the power of a Nephilim...a sad mistake for him. He only realised it moments before he died." Mal's voice cut through the dying laughter hitting home. The smile died on the Fallen Angels' face to be replaced by cold fury. In an instant he had taken off from the ground screaming, "You will pay for that comment." In a second he was twenty feet above the ground stretching both hands in Malchediel's direction. Lightning bolts surged from his fingertips but Malchediel was ready and sprang to his left and at the same moment unfurled his own wings. The bolts of fire buried deep into the grass scorching and burning before disappearing, dampened by the early morning dew. "You were clearly not a Warrior before your fall." Malchediel sneered as he too took to the air, flying quickly around and behind his enemy. Before he knew what was happening the Fallen Angel had been hit by Malchediel's own Bolt hurling him head over heels to land some twenty feet away dazed and bleeding, his wings now crumpled and useless. He screamed in pain and fury calling to his Demons to attack the Nephilim. Malchediel swooped back down to the ground as half a dozen of the Demons surged forwards. Instantly the Nephilim defended themselves using whatever weapons they preferred. Within seconds all the attacking Demons had been killed and were disintegrating, leaving only charred grass and flakes of burned flesh to float downwards.

Malchediel was back at Amy's side, "You need to use your telepathy again Amy. Cause another distraction. We are greatly outnumbered. Do it now...I will cover you." He stepped in front of her as she concentrated on the baying Demons now being egged on by the Fallen. She sensed that they were all being controlled by the different Angels present so she couldn't delve into all their minds at the same time. She worked on the few at the front of the group. As before she saw that their greatest fear was the Angel who was controlling them. She concentrated hard trying to ignore the noise going on around her as some of the Demons incited by their controllers attacked the few Nephilim present. It was difficult focussing with all the mayhem around her but she finally succeeded in planting thoughts in some of the creatures. Half a dozen or so halted their attack and turned instead upon the Angels standing behind them. Working on their fear, she started causing chaos as those at the front turned trampling others behind them in their frenzied attempt to free themselves from their masters. The Fallen Angels, at first so confident and self-assured now saw their puppets in disarray. The attack was turning into a rout. The few Nephilim seeing the tide turning began cheering, moving forward using their weapons on the confused Demons. Malchediel turned to see Amy swaying with the effort of keeping her mind focussed on controlling the Demons. He knew that she would not be able to keep this up much longer. He wanted to take her in his arms, to support her, to tell her to stop draining herself but they were winning now. He had to let her finish what she had started. He turned back to the battle joining the Nephilim in taking down as many Demons as he could. From the far side he could see that the Fallen, trying to protect themselves were doing exactly the same thing. He could almost feel sorry for the mindless creatures caught in the middle as they died and disintegrated one after the other. The Nephilim themselves suffered only minor injuries.

He wasn't sure how long it took him to become aware of the earth tremors beneath his feet. For some minutes he put it down to the sounds of battle, the falling bodies of the Demons, the surge of bodies edging forwards. Then he became aware of the Fallen Angels backing away from the anomaly that was still gaping wide behind them. He recognised the look of fear passing between them. Then he felt the earth lurch beneath him. He staggered, planting his feet firmly apart as the ground rolled and heaved beneath him.

What was going on?

Abruptly billows of red smoke belched from the anomaly rolling out engulfing the Fallen Angels as they attempted to distance themselves from the commotion. A roaring ensued as the ground lurched. The red smoke grew thicker spewing from the aberration clouding Malchediel's view. With his eyes riveted on the roiling, billowing smoke he now became aware of the sounds also spilling from the anomaly. It sounded like distant thunder rolling on and on becoming louder by the second. The earth still heaved toppling some of the Nephilim and Fallen Angels alike. Then with one great belch a final whoosh of smoke gushed forth bringing with it an appalling stench of sulphur. Amy gasped, her concentration broken as everyone tried to see through the slowly dissipating red fog. She stepped sideways so that her view wasn't blocked by Malchediel and stared through the haze. The fighting had stopped. The Demons were turning this way and that utterly confused. No one was giving them any orders and they were too stupid to know what to do without instruction. The lurching ground slowly stilled and at last the red smoke began to clear. Amy heard Malchediel's sharp intake of breath followed by a strangled expletive in his own tongue. She turned to him, "What! What is it? What can you see?"

"Hell...I can see Hell." Without looking at her he sought her hand. Catching it, he pulled her close putting his arm around her shoulders as if this gesture alone would save her from what he could see.

She turned to look back at the Anomaly that was now beginning to become visible again through the smoke. She heard Malchediel talking quietly in his Angelic language. Unable to understand his words she knew that he was praying. A feeling of dread filtered through her...This was bad. Very bad.

Chapter Thirteen

Through the rapidly dissolving smoke she could now see a figure. She blinked trying to clear the tears caused by the sulphur fumes and stared at the figure. It was a man, no not a man, he was an Angel. She could now see his wings. She caught her breath. She had only seen wings that black once before and they had belonged to Asmodeus. "Oh my God." She whispered watching him step forward to survey the scene before him.

"No...not God my love... Lucifer." She barely heard Malchediel's voice.

She couldn't take her eyes from the most notorious Fallen Angel of all time. "But he's beautiful Mal." she whispered back.

Malchediel made a harsh derisive sound, "But his heart is ugly."

Almost casually, Lucifer strolled forward stopping regarding the bewildered Demons between him and the Nephilim. He shook his head as though disappointed. Then he looked over their heads scanning the Nephilim, his eyes alighting on Amy in Malchediel's arms. For a moment he stared at them and then with a sweep of his arm he caused the intervening Demons to completely disappear. One second they were there, hovering uncertainly and the next they had vanished. Amy let out an exclamation and Mal's arm tightened around her in warning. Lucifer walked forward across the space where the Demons had stood approaching them both. In the few seconds that it took for him to come before them, Amy assessed him. His wings though deepest black were amazing, silky, shining in the early morning sunlight. The tips brushed the ground as he walked. He was tall, broad shouldered and clad in what appeared to be a Roman Centurion's uniform. The short tunic reached his mid -thigh. He was wearing a metal breast plate, Vambraces and Greaves and boots of the finest leather.

He looked magnificent. His face was perfectly proportioned and those eyes were the deepest green. His hair like all the Angels she had seen so far was worn long. The auburn tresses framing his perfect face, falling silkily to his shoulders.

Surely Satan shouldn't look this hot? *Where were the horns? The tail?*

He surveyed Amy carefully, his head to one side. He caught the movement of Malchediel sereptisously attempting to ease Amy behind him. He frowned and she saw the anger flash across his face. His eyes locked on Malchediel's and she was horrified to see her lover slowly sink down to one knee, unable to resist Lucifer's telepathic power over him.

How was Lucifer doing this?

"Stop it!" she cried, "Please stop whatever it is you're doing." As the words left her mouth she felt fearful. No one spoke to Lucifer like that surely?

She was surprised to see a smile touch his lips as he turned his gaze back to her. Malchediel was still on bended knee as if in supplication, waiting for Lucifer to bestow some sort of honour upon him.

Then the Prince of Darkness spoke. "You are so like her. After all this time...I see her in your face."

Amy stared at him...*Was he referring to her? What did he mean?*

"What is your given name?" He spoke again.

Before she could answer, the Fallen Angel who lay injured a few yards away called out, "She is the Nephilim responsible for the death of Asmodeus my Lord."

Without taking his eyes from her face Lucifer asked, "And what do you propose I do about that Azazel?"

"She must die." Was the answer.

Amy felt Malchediel's hand tighten around her fingers as the blood drained from her face.

Lucifer's lip curled into the hint of a smile, "Really?"

Amy felt her knees give way as she sank down next to Malchediel. So this was to be her fate, to die here in the early morning light on the dew soaked grass of an old Manor House. Would they kill Malchediel too? And what about her fellow Nephilim officers standing around witnessing this bizarre scenario? She closed her eyes. This was where it was all going to end then. The Fallen had won.

She felt two cold hands gently cup her face. "You're wrong Azazel. She will not die..."

"But my Lord..." The wounded Angel grimaced as he struggled to rise, his left wing hanging at a crazy angle.

"Silence!"

Amy opened her eyes at Lucifer's steely command. His face was inches from hers and it occurred to her that the colour of their hair was identical. How strange. She dragged her eyes from his to turn to Malchediel kneeling alongside her and she had an irresistible, hysterical desire to laugh at her predicament holding hands with her Angel lover whilst having her face cupped by the Prince of Darkness.

'You are thinking it strange that we should have the same hair colour?' Lucifer's lips didn't move but she heard his voice clearly in her head. He had read her mind. She nodded.

'Not so strange...Amy...that is your name is it not?'

"Yes." She whispered.

'And you are the one that cut short the life of Asmodeus?' The question entered her mind with no hint of anger. He could have been asking if she wanted sugar in her tea, but this was Lucifer, the font of all evil. His even tone could belie his intentions of what to do to her. Squaring her shoulders she looked him in the eye and showing a courage that she was certainly not feeling answered, "Yes and he deserved to die. He killed my parents...and countless others." She added. She barely heard Malchediel's sharp intake of breath. This could be it...This could be where Lucifer struck her down. She waited.

Lucifer let go of her chin as he straightened. "Believe me Amy; I knew nothing of what you say." He was speaking now not using thoughts to communicate with her. He sounded almost sad and both she and Malchediel looked at him in bewilderment. "I have only learned of your grievances against him since his death. I would have punished him myself had I known."

"MY LORD!" Azazel's voice rang out in horror at Lucifer's words.

"Azazel…if you speak once more without my permission you will regret it."

Azazel's lips clamped shut as he sank back down to the ground, lips working angrily but his words were inaudible.

Lucifer turned his attention back to Amy. He smiled at her expression of astonishment. *'You may well be puzzled Amy. You were not expecting this from the Prince of Darkness, Satan, Beelzebub or whatever other name you humans attach to me, were you?'* He sighed, a world weary sigh. *'I was not always evil personified'.* He eased himself down once more, kneeling before her. Taking a strand of her hair he stroked the length of the tress between his fingers. Malchediel tried to shift his position, but all he was able to achieve was a look of anger directed at Lucifer for daring to touch the girl at his side.

"Oh calm yourself Malchediel I will not harm her."

Amy felt Lucifer's eyes appraising her, his palms cool against her cheeks.

'Do you love him?' The thought came so unexpectedly into her mind that she felt herself blush.

"Yes." She answered quietly.

"Hmmm. I remember those feelings."

Amy couldn't believe what she was hearing. Lucifer professing his love for someone?

The silence lengthened, everyone waiting for what would come next. Only Amy had been privy to Lucifer's thoughts. To everyone else present, his intermittent spoken words didn't make any sense.

'Her name was Naamah.' He continued to stroke the auburn tress through his fingers seeming to be lost in thoughts of long ago. Then his eyes held hers as he continued sending his thoughts to her.

'I met her after I fell to earth. At first I thought she was just another human. Someone to enjoy. A brief interlude, a balm to my anger with Him who dared to cast me out.' His eyes once again became unfocussed staring out past Amy's shoulder into the distance. She waited. Eventually he went on. 'She was beautiful, gentle and caring and for the first time ever, I fell in love.'

"Why are you telling me this?" she asked quietly. His eyes were drawn back to her face.

"I think you are very like her." He answered using his voice. Those close enough strained to hear his words. 'All you have inherited from me is the colour of your hair.'

WHAM...she felt as though she had been slammed in the gut with a baseball bat

"WHAT! What!" she exploded, then remembering that there were inquisitive ears listening she switched to telepathy, 'Are you saying that I am descended from you and Naam...' She couldn't remember his partner's name.

He gave a short laugh, "Naamah..." he finished for her, "Yes Amy that is exactly what I am saying."

Her hand flew to her mouth in shock. "How long ago are we talking about?"

'We are talking in terms of millennia. Naamah was a human girl. Such a short life.' He sighed. 'I have never forgotten her.' He let the lock of hair that he had been fingering drop to Amy's shoulder.

"I am tired of this conflict." He stood up glancing at the six Fallen Angels then he looked down at Malchediel whilst drawing his hand through the air before him. At once Malchediel, freed from the invisible restraints that had held him on bended knee stood up gathering Amy to his side. Lucifer turned to Malchediel and spoke, "He won't forgive will he? I could slay every human on this accursed planet and it would make no difference to Him. I and my brethren would still be banished. Am I right Malchediel?"

"I fear that is the case. I too am a Fallen Angel. I think none of us will ever see our former home again."

"Then continuing this global battle is truly pointless." Lucifer looked around him. "Why lay waste to all this beauty? If we are forced to live here for all eternity then we should preserve what He created."

He turned once again to the six Fallen Angels, "Take him with you." He said indicating the injured Azazel, "I will join you shortly." He waited while they made their way back through the anomaly assisting   Azazel who was limping badly. Once alone with Malchediel and Amy he spoke again, "Malchediel, a word alone." Leaving Amy to stare after them, he led Malchediel away to where they would not be overheard. "Whilst touching Amy's hair, I sensed that she had been injured recently."

Malchediel frowned, '*Where was this going?*' "Yes a Demon spine embedded itself in her neck."

Lucifer's eyes widened but Malchediel hurried on, "I asked Raphael to heal her."

"And he did?"

"Only after Michael intervened. He agreed that Raphael could treat her."

A slow smile spread across Lucifer's handsome face. "I wonder why that was so?" He eyed Malchediel wondering whether to share what was on his mind. Then he went on, "There was a time when Michael and I were the closest of friends..." he kicked the turf with his soft leather boot before looking back into Malchediel's face. "Seeing Amy was quite a shock for me. I will let her explain the reason for that once you are alone together. I suspect that Michael also saw something familiar about the colour of her hair. I believe he intervened on her behalf with Raphael for old times' sake." He looked over to the dozen or so Nephilim standing staring back at them. A slow smile spread across his features. "I have a reputation to uphold...I suggest you stand back."

As Malchediel strode back over to where Amy was standing Lucifer drew himself up and to the horror of the

Lightning Source UK Ltd.
Milton Keynes UK
UKOW03f0832120914

238421UK00001B/6/P